A MYSTERY for THOREAU

Being the Story of a Young Gentleman of the Press Who Dutifully Reported on the Strange and Bizarre Happenings in Concord, Massachusetts, in the Year of 1846. How He Dealt with Educated Transcendentalists and Lunatics. How He Became Involved with a Cruel and Savage Crime, and What Extreme Steps He Took to Ascertain the Identity of the Callous Perpetrator and Bring Justice to Bear. With Much Edifying Matter Concerning the Customs, Beliefs, and Discoveries to Which That Distressing Calamity Gave Rise

Kin Platt

A MYSTERY FOR
THOREAU

Foreword by
Christopher J. Platt

Farrar, Straus and Giroux • New York

www.fsgkidsbooks.com

Library of Congress Cataloging-in-Publication Data

Platt, Kin.

A mystery for Thoreau / Kin Platt ; foreword by Christopher J. Platt.— 1st ed.

p.   cm.

Summary: In 1846 Concord, Massachusetts, sixteen-year-old Oliver Puckle, a reporter for his uncle's newspaper, investigates a woman's murder, aided by the tracking skills of his Algonquin friend, Charley Bigbow, and the deductive skills of Henry David Thoreau.

ISBN-13: 978-0-374-35337-7

ISBN-10: 0-374-35337-9

[1. Journalists—Fiction.   2. Murder—Fiction.   3. Thoreau, Henry David, 1817–1862—Fiction.   4. Algonquin Indians—Fiction.   5. Indians of North America—Massachusetts—Fiction.   6. Concord (Mass.)—History—19th century—Fiction.   7. Mystery and detective stories.]   I. Title.

PZ7.P7125Mxt 2008

[Fic]—dc22

2007040115

Interior artwork © 2008 by Danijel Zezelj

FOREWORD

When my father's first book, *The Blue Man*, was published by Harper & Brothers in 1961, we were living in Santa Monica, California, in a house rented from a UCLA professor. The place was a mansion compared with our home on Long Island, and with that, and other California-size expenses, my father was struggling to support the family. But he had come to California the year before, intent on finding gainful employment before he sent for us to join him. Apparently, not having us underfoot gave him the time and working conditions he needed to produce a novel. Never reluctant to try something new to earn a living, he was, by now, used to not giving us the details of all the ventures he undertook that didn't succeed. If the book had flopped, we might never have known of its existence, either.

For decades, Kin Platt had made his living in cartoons and comic books. After working throughout the 1930s as a writer for radio stars such as George Burns and Jack Benny, he landed work writing for theatrical cartoons produced by Walt Disney and Walter Lantz. He was writing and drawing for the nascent comic book industry by the late 1930s. One of his 1940s comic characters for Exciting Comics, The Mask, was a blind district attorney who had a secret identity as a masked crime fighter, much as in Marvel Comics' *Daredevil*, which debuted in 1964. It's interesting that Stan Lee, creator of *Daredevil* and so many other titles at Marvel, had worked with my father in the early 1940s at Timely Comics, the forerunner to Marvel. Kin Platt also created the world's first animal superhero, Super Mouse, in 1942. In 1947, he began writing, later both writing and drawing, the *Mr. and Mrs.* comic strip created by Clare Briggs in 1924 for the *New York Herald Tribune*. He would continue with that classic comic strip until 1963. In the 1950s, Kin Platt also began writing for DC Comics, home of *Superman* and *Batman*. But the comics he wrote were not about superheroes, they were about TV stars: *The Adventures of Dean Martin & Jerry Lewis* (later, just *Jerry Lewis*), *Bob Hope*, and *Phil Silvers*, to name but a few comic book titles you never heard of. Several years later he would be writing stories for the animated cartoons of Hanna-Barbera—*Top Cat*, *The Flintstones*, *Jonny Quest*, *The Yogi Bear Show*, *The Jetsons*. All fun stuff, sure, but none of it paid much.

Books were a natural next step for a professional storyteller. But the first major review, from *Library Journal*, was a disaster. The reviewer was upset that the story revolved around a boy who had picked up a gun, taken a car that wasn't his, and was driving cross-country (without a driver's license!) to hunt down a mysterious blue man he thought had killed his aunt and uncle. With what's available to young people today, in books, graphic novels, movies, video games, and on television, the reviewer's qualms now seem very quaint. But in 1961, that one review could have been the kiss of death.

Other reviewers would eventually come to see the finer aspects of the book, especially the heroic nature of a scared teenager on a quest, suddenly forced to make life-or-death decisions. But I wanted to help, and I couldn't wait for the good reviews to come. The next day, after school, I stuffed my backpack full of copies of *The Blue Man*, tore the "Branch Library" page out of the local Yellow Pages, hopped on my bike, and set off on a quest of my own.

Over the next several weeks, I visited every branch of the public library in Santa Monica and West Los Angeles. I'd introduce myself to the librarians and urge them to take a free copy to read, then decide for themselves if they wanted it on their shelves, despite what *Library Journal* had said about it. Not surprisingly, all the librarians took me up on the offer. Fortunately, they nearly all called back to say how much they loved the book, and that they were going to order additional copies. The librarians—and librarians around the country whom I never met—were the heroes in my quest. Their acceptance ignited and sustained my father's career as an author. In fact, some of those copies, now tattered and torn, are still on the shelves in Santa Monica libraries.

Kin Platt would eventually go on to publish thirty-three more books under his own name, and three others under the pseudonym Nick West. He wrote in more genres than any author I know of (at least ten). After his death, in 2003, my cousin Cheryl—long my father's favorite niece—and I joined forces to bring his books to a new generation. We eventually helped a young man set up a tiny "niche" publishing house because the first book he wanted to publish was *The Blue Man*.

Months later, we had printed up several hundred new copies, and I brought them to a major convention in New York City for publishers, librarians, and booksellers. Our tiny booth was in the southernmost aisle, with a lot of other small publishers. The big firms were bunched in the center of the building, hundreds of yards away. That was the high-rent district, and we were definitely low-rent. However, I'd made it a point to position us across from the Librarians' Lounge. I hung a garish sign with a big pink heart: WE ♥ LIBRARIANS. When I saw a librarian, I'd steer her (they were mostly women) to our table and tell her the saga of the heroic librarians who had supported my father's work. I'd thank her, press a copy of *The Blue Man* into her hands with a shopping bag full of other little goodies, and ask her to remember us when the book was formally published that summer.

On Day 2 of the convention, Cheryl called me at the booth from her home in the Oregon woods. She was watching a panel discussion from the convention on C-Span, from the other side of the building, apparently. The panelists were editors, publishers, and agents who told how eager they were for great young adult books. Cheryl read me their names and companies, and later that day, I headed for the center of the building to leave them all copies of *The Blue Man* and the materials I'd given the librarians. In each book, I enclosed my card with a brief handwritten note. Only one of the six panelists—Wesley Adams, an executive editor at Farrar, Straus and Giroux in New York— responded. Several weeks later, he e-mailed me, asking what I wanted from him. Since my tiny niche publisher had, by this time, literally vanished, I replied, "Simple! Let's republish all my father's books for young adults and get rich!"

Wes had the grace to sound intrigued while evincing moderate embarrassment that anyone had seen him on TV. But he explained that, for FSG to consider publishing a dead author with whom they have no history, it might make sense to start with something previously unavailable. He asked if I had anything else, unpublished. I did. After my father's death, I'd spent a week cleaning out his apartment, shipping a lot to Howard Gotlieb at the Boston University library, where he maintains the Kin Platt Collection. But I'd kept boxes full of manuscripts, and Cheryl had others, which eventually yielded nearly two dozen unpublished works. Wes told me to take the summer and read them all and then, after Labor Day, to send him the best of the lot. By September, I had mailed him two candidates: this story and a Japanese-themed fable about a young boy and a vengeful dragon.

When Wes finally had the opportunity to read them, he quickly passed on the fable, but he was very enthusiastic about *A Mystery for Thoreau*, my father's only historical novel. Over the months that followed, we kept in touch. Wes shared the manuscript with his colleagues, looking for feedback that would help in the acquisition process. Eventually, he decided to solicit the opinion of an outside reader who was not only a literature professor at a college here in New York but also a Thoreau scholar. The professor liked it, too, and I think that must have been the tipping point.

Kin Platt often went where other authors feared to tread. He wrote of tough situations, tough times, and tough neighborhoods. His youngsters often talked in the language of the streets, and their dialogue and actions would scandalize reviewers for three decades. This book is different, and surely was written after he'd mellowed a bit. And if he wrote another historical novel, I have yet to find it. So this is one-of-a-kind in many ways. But, then, so was the author.

—Christopher J. Platt

A MYSTERY FOR THOREAU

Of Concord and Its Inhabitants, Including Myself, Oliver Puckle

In 1635, the early settlers pushed their livestock past the swamps and forests this far and decided it would do. Simon Willard, our founder, then proclaimed it to be called Concord, to mean the town of agreeing men.

Now, after a little over two hundred years, we have become a thriving mill town with a population of two thousand. We have our own newspaper, the *Concord Freeman*, owned and published by my uncle Rufus Puckle, to whom I am in hire. Along with my aunt Martha, Uncle Rufus has reared me since my birth. My mother died soon after of complications, and I never knew my father, either, as he had already gone fainthearted, deserting her, unable to cherish the notion of parenthood.

My mother was Emily Puckle, younger sister to Uncle Rufus, and in his wrath at my father's abandoning us, my uncle denied me his name and made me a Puckle, too. That was sixteen years ago. I have learned since that my father's name was Desmond

Defoe, but I am still a Puckle. I have seen neither hide nor hair of my light-footed sire in the ensuing years. I would not care to make his acquaintance, although I'm told I would know him at once by his breath and gait, as Desmond Defoe consumed vast quantities of whatever was available in the taverns.

My uncle's Puckle forebears in England were notorious for speaking their minds, and consequently several lost their estates along with their heads for their zealous moral and reformist notions. The family traits have not been lost in passage, and the *Concord Freeman* affords my uncle ample space for his voice on all matters concerning the conduct of government or its citizens. It is my duty to seek out and collect the news of local origin, whether what transpires at the Social Circle in Concord, the antislavery societies, or temperance societies seems significant or not. Barn burnings, fights in taverns, jailings, or even a heifer's birth—they are all mine to observe and report upon.

We have farming and a manufacturer of lead pipe. A shoe factory with more than a dozen employees. A cotton mill that hires thirty girls, three boys, and nine men. There are six warehouses, a bindery, two sawmills, two gristmills, and a powder mill. There are makers of pencils, clocks, hats, bellows, guns, bricks, barrels, and harnesses. There are several taverns for the teamsters whose wagons are horse drawn or pulled by oxen.

We have a courthouse in the center of town for meetings, and the Concord Lyceum puts on lectures and poetry readings. There is a public school and the Academy for older, wealthier students preparing for college.

We are sixteen miles west of Boston, which is four hours by stage, although our new Fitchburg Railroad has shortened the time to one hour and the price of fare by half.

We have nine miles of river; the Sudbury joined by the Assabet becomes the Concord and flows north to the Middlesex Canal between Lowell and Boston, then on to join the Merrimack, which enters the sea up at Newburyport and Plum Island. Boats with wood and cargo come from Maine and Boston through the canal. We have one road to Boston, the Cambridge Turnpike, as well as the Lincoln Road, going east by Walden Pond, the Sudbury Road, the Old Lexington Road, the Union Turnpike west to the Berkshires, and the Old Carlisle Road north to New Hampshire.

The village center is a small green square with rows of shops on a former mill dam built on a brook flowing from the meadow of Ralph Waldo Emerson, our leading public figure. The town and village is nearly twenty-four square miles. There are several long tree-shaded streets, and the houses are mostly white. The town merges to country on the one side, and on the other the lawns stretch to the marshes and river.

In our waters can be found mussels, muskrats, fish, turtles, and wild fowl. Indian arrowheads of flint can be found along the banks.

Just two miles from the square are fox trails. There are woodchucks, chickadees, shorebirds, and forest birds. We have swamps with maple, spruce, and, in between, shrub oak and huckleberry, cedar and prickly juniper. The woods are thick with pine, ash, aspen, beech, birch, black willow, chestnut and elm, hemlock, hickory, oak, scarlet oak, pitch pine, white birch, and willow.

For mountains, we have Wachusett, a day hike west of Concord. Also Mount Misery. We have Bateman's Pond, Flint's Pond, Goose Pond, White Pond, and Walden Pond. We have three swamps, Yellow Birch Swamp, Beck Stow's, and Miles.

There are still some Indians living among us, some Negro families, and the Irish, who stayed on after building the railroad and now live in their mean little shanties.

Our village is home to many of distinction. They are mostly of a philosophical bent, transcendentalism being their preferred way to look at the world with new eyes. God-like men, such as Mr. Emerson, who left his Boston pulpit when his wife died, then settled here and married his new wife, Lidian. Inspired talkers like Bronson Alcott, spewing words with torrential force, dedicated to the spirit and man's upward path, unable to harm a mosquito, potato bug, or any living creature, so averse to the slavery of domestic animals, he plows his fields without horse or oxen.

There is the reclusive David Henry Thoreau, who inverted his names to Henry David after graduating from Harvard, now living on Emerson's acres at Walden Pond, observing nature.

There are our intelligent women, Abolitionists all. Mrs. Elizabeth Hoar, Mrs. Sarah Ripley, Margaret Fuller, editor of *The Dial*, until recently an organ for Emerson and his transcendentalists. The mother of Thoreau, Cynthia Dunbar, and his artistic sister Helen.

We have the eccentrics, such as the notorious Joseph Palmer, who was jailed for refusing to cut his beard, flaunting it now, surely the most luxuriant ever grown by man. We have some Millerites from Pittsfield who waited on a hill there for the world to end as foretold by their leader, William Miller. We have Samuel Larned, who has subsisted one year on crackers alone, the next on apples. And Bronson Alcott himself, who lately ran the failed commune at Fruitlands, refusing to use sheep as slavery, thereby eliminating wool clothing, growing silkworms instead, then creating garments from their fiber.

Mr. Thoreau, too, might be included. He dislikes black clothing, never shines his boots, wears his trousers too long, carries his luggage in brown paper or a red piece of cloth, goes without overcoat, gloves, or underwear, and never did learn to tie a proper knot, so that his shoelaces always come untied. He will never answer a direct question and walks always with his head down, observing the ground. He avoids all attempts at conversation but is more forthcoming in his woods, speaking there to squirrels, woodchucks, and birds, who sometimes respond. The hermetic retreat he has built on Walden Pond is in plain view from the main road, and he returns to the village every day.

Until his recent move to Salem, the author Nathaniel Hawthorne lived here, so handsome people stopped to stare. He wore only dark clothing and a blue frock, skulking to taverns, his hat pulled low, living with his bride, Sophia Peabody, at the Old Manse behind black ash trees, near the old Revolutionary battleground. Emerson shuddered at Hawthorne's bleak visions, but, when the Hawthornes moved in on their wedding day in 1842, they found a flower and vegetable garden, freshly dug and planted by Thoreau.

Without Mr. Emerson, Concord would be a sorry place, a village of embattled strivers who vie for attention. Each is admittedly of sound purpose, but all agree without argument or envy that Emerson is the supreme kingpin that binds them all together. His effect on whomever he shall meet is akin to idolatry and instant subservience, although he makes no attempt to dominate in word or manner. It is as if he has descended to us from a higher plane, one we shall never know nor hope to achieve, as close to a living god as can be imagined.

Tall and slender, if not painfully thin, he carries his long, narrow head on an elongated, stalklike neck without any pretense of pride, yet still conveys his own majesty. His shoulders slope to an amazing degree, and he carries one higher than the other. His eyes are the clearest blue one could imagine, and they can be singularly penetrating and piercing in conversation. His nose is an overgenerous combination of bone and cartilage but suits the somber expression set by his lips, which curve easily in animated discourse. He walks at a quick pace and seems tireless.

He is friend to all and responsive backer of any who need support. He has published only two sets of his essays, yet has revolutionized thought in New England. His lectures are always an inspiration, and he commands the highest fees and largest audiences of any public speaker. I love my uncle Rufus, but my heart twitters when I'm near Emerson.

His aunt Mary Moody sometimes lives at the Emerson house, the old Coolidge residence on the Cambridge Turnpike to Boston, a large two-story with Doric porticoes front and side, set comfortably in two acres about a mile from the square. She is a dwarf, about four feet three, with a shaggy crop of yellow hair usually covered by her mobcap. The daughter of the former minister of Concord who died in the Revolution, Miss Mary Moody has the most acerbic wit and the most far-reaching, brilliant mind in Concord. To dare her in ordinary conversation is most daunting, as she suffers no fools and prides herself on withering insult.

Of the five Emerson boys, Waldo, as he prefers to be called, is her favorite. She taught Mr. Emerson to read and write, and to be proud of his lineage as the sixth generation of sovereign ruling priests.

She exists on only bread and water, courts death, and has stitched her own shroud to live in. She wears it as a nightgown and a day gown, even while cantering her horse on the streets of Concord, with only her sham for cover. Her bed is made in the form of a coffin, and she speaks hopefully of worms as most valuable companions. She is born to command and dictate, and yearns for the flaming death of the saints.

There is one other of great notoriety in Concord town, and I must not neglect her in my story. The lady I refer to is Miss Hetta Bird, our local madwoman, given to visions.

Miss Hetta is birdlike in her movements, remindful of the masterful Edgar Allan Poe's "Raven," which I have been fortunate to read recently in an old issue of *The American Review*. Hetta, too, flutters and croaks, and, gray hair notwithstanding, is as dark and demonic as the ingenious poet's own imagined creature.

The passing years have not added to Hetta's derangement; I

remember her so since early childhood. All of us were frightened of this addled scarecrow woman, who darted at us suddenly from thickets in the forest, sometimes shouting wild gibberish. She would flail her long, skinny arms with odd, jerky movements, screaming imprecations, or confound us utterly by suddenly bursting into song, lifting her tattered skirt, and dancing around some birch or pine, skipping like a child.

There were terrifying stories about Hetta. She ate rats, she ate chickens raw, she ate children. Could this be? we asked ourselves with pounding hearts, and if so, who among us would be next? We knew our families would never be able to find us if we were unlucky enough to be caught by her, then dragged to her foul home in the swamplands. It was a tiny hut of rotted boards, abandoned years back by a local hunter and trapper, fronted by dense thicket and scrub oak. It had a dirt floor, no windows, and one day when she was gone, we ventured inside, saw the litter of bones scattered around the hearth, and fled, horror-struck.

My playmates, all with living parents, whether farmers or townspeople, had been encouraged to fear and believe the worst of this spectral faerie of the woods. When I asked my uncle and aunt if the stories were true, my uncle looked coldly at me and snorted, "Humbug, Oliver! Only a fool believes in hearsay." My dear aunt, too sweet and trusting to believe a viper would bite, could only sigh and murmur, "Poor lost soul."

There were her dark visions many had sworn to, revelations coming to pass. Foreseen blights on family or crop. It was only the underlying good temperament of the Concord citizens that dissuaded them from damning her completely and calling her a witch.

We soon found Hetta harmless and, as we grew, with the callous brutality and bravado of children, would tease and sometimes taunt her. There were times when she would seem to welcome our catcalls as affectionate dialogue, and would smile and scream her own responses as though we were family. But her moods would change, and sometimes she would hear us out dumbly, stare and shake her head in confusion, and suddenly turn and dart away as if in fear for her life. At such times we would feel a brief swelling of triumph, but this would be short-lived; soon we would be assailed by conscience, our laughter and jesting stilled. Deep in our young hearts, there was no escaping our fondness for this pathetic, addled soul. She was as precious to us as some dotty aunt or grandmother, and we would make amends over and again by secret gifts of wild apples and berries left at her doorstep. Sometimes, too, we left flowers for her and were rewarded some future day by seeing Hetta flit wraithlike through the high meadow grass wearing our fading garlands in her straggly, unkempt hair. We would nod to each other then, rejoicing in our redemption, proud of our innate goodness.

Hetta rarely ventured into the village. When she did, ladies reacted to her filthy and verminous presence as if fleeing the plague. They would bolt to the opposite side of the street, those with offspring dragging their tots by the hair if need be, to avoid the possibility of contamination. Most of the male townspeople were similarly chary and apprehensive and, if unwilling to demonstrate their fears by open and precipitous flight, would prudently hide behind the elms on Main Street until Hetta's course could be estimated.

The main shops are on the village square built on the old Mill Dam over a stream flowing past Emerson's meadow. Here are our two banks, the post office, my uncle's *Concord Freeman*, and the rest. The wood-fronted grocery and country store of Walcott and Holden, where traders tie their horses and meet to gossip. Asa Collier's watch store, the boot shop of Jonas Hastings, and that of Alvan Pratt, who repairs skates. Next is Reynolds's Apothecary. All are known as hiding dens for runaway slaves, as is Mr. Thoreau's own hut.

Hetta's incursions led her most often to the apothecary. She would wait outside, peering through the tiny panes until all customers had gone, then venture in. It was barter that brought her here. She made her own ink, steeping maple bark and oak in indigo and alum. In exchange, Arthur Reynolds would fill a bag for her of licorice sticks. I have tried her ink myself and found it better than most commercial products available. Mr. Thoreau likes its quality and brightness, and is not above barter, either, exchanging some of the good pencils his father makes, sometimes with his help, for Hetta's jars of ink.

Perhaps no more would be made of Hetta's presence in Concord town were it not for our recent chance meeting. It was that which inspired me to write this account, after she summarily involved me in one of her darkest visions.

Of the Encounter on the
Old Lexington Road

I t was early of a Friday morning, the air clear, with the morning sun embracing all. The old road was clear of teamsters and farmers hauling their hay. I was walking along its center, my head down in the manner of Mr. Thoreau, seeing only the dust under my boots and wondering what he ever saw in this manner that I never could, although I would have sworn my eyes were as keen.

Alerted by an odd hissing sound, I looked up, and to my surprise, the remarkably attired Hetta materialized at my side. She had somehow arranged her person in a costume so weird that, trained as I am to observe details and thence translate them into newsworthy copy, I was rendered impotent of thought. Slowly, then, the details fell into place as my eyes twitched and turned to encompass all.

She wore one berry-stained boot alongside a mud-caked shoe. Her long skirt trailing in the dust was a tattered blanket wound around herself, tied with strings. Her blouse was a soiled pillow-case, with holes cut out for her arms. A strip of red rag was arranged upon her head like a kerchief, through which pro-truded clusters of long-stemmed flowers. Her remarkably bony face was oddly free of wrinkles, considering her age.

Long, skeletal fingers clutched at my arm, and her nasal voice croaked close to my ear. She was agitated, and her breath spoke of much mulberry wine.

"Hearken, young general," she said. "Methinks I saw a red-coat scurry into the barn yonder of good farmer Bonder. Where are your men?"

Hetta's wild, staring eyes showed no sign of recognition, al-though she had seen me since my early childhood. But it had been many years since I last ventured into her thicket of swamp fern and thorn to deposit stinkweeds at her door and smear bird droppings on its crude latch meant as a doorknob.

I patted her thin hand, unwilling to offend by an attempted withdrawal. It may have been impossible, in any event, as her nails were as sharp as the talons of a hawk. "Miss Hetta," I said, looking into her watery gray eyes, "the British have long been gone."

Her brows lifted in astonishment. "What d'ye say?"

I nodded in comforting fashion. "We drove them off seventy years ago. The last of them were in retreat over this very Lexing-ton Road."

"Wal, I vum!" she said, shaking her head.

"It's true as I stand here," I continued. "And I'm no general but a humble news gatherer working at yon shop on the green.

My name is Oliver Puckle, Miss Hetta. Ollie to my friends, among which enshrined circle I hope to include your own dear self one day."

She stared vacantly, nodding and smiling as my hand patted hers. Suddenly she drew back, removed her hand, and jabbed a long grimed finger before my nose.

"I know ye now, ye snotted devil," she shrilled. "You be the one throwed the rotted apple at me down in Hubbard's Path. Spoiled me fancy new frock, ye did, blast yer bones."

Brought up short by this uncanny recall, I pursed my lips, whistling softly. "Miss Hetta, that was near ten years ago. I am truly sorry for that and the many egregious wrongs I've done you. I would truly welcome your forgiveness of all my idle and mean childhood pranks."

She wagged her head. "Yer saying it be ten years back that it was? And the Hoosians be all gone, too?"

I blinked and recovered, finally fathoming her reference to the German mercenary soldiers who fought for the British. "The Hessians, too, yes."

Her head cocked to one side, birdlike again. "There was one o' them was sweet on me, ye know. Rolled his eye when he passed, dressed all magnificent, he was. I wanted to follow, but me mum, she slapped me hard. I was only ten, said she, it could wait a year."

"Miss Hetta, your mum was quite right," I said. "Those Hessians all went back to Saxony, if they left these shores alive. Their dukes and princes would then hire them out to fight elsewhere. You might have been a child bride widow there in a foreign land whose language would not be clear to you. Here in Concord, at least, you are among friends, some such as myself anxious to know you better."

She listened patiently, then rubbed her head. "I do beg patience, m'lord. All is of a mix here. Lost I am in too many days. What year is it now?"

"Dear Miss Hetta, I'll bring you thoroughly up to date. Today is Friday, the twenty-fourth of July, and the year is 1846."

She bent her head and mumbled as she counted her fingers. "That is a fair lot to count," she said, giving it up. "The numbers have no meaning for me. All I know is what I see before me and hear in my head."

"Then what have you seen or heard lately, Miss Hetta? I am in the business of gathering news. Although trivial to you, it might be of interest to our readers." I jingled some coins in my pocket. "I might persuade my uncle to pay for a good story. Perhaps have a sketch of you alongside."

She stamped her boot impatiently. " 'Tis you I come to see. I've a vision for ye."

"A vision?" I said, frowning. "My uncle does not permit me to indulge in fanciful prose, Miss Hetta. He is a stubborn man, interested only in verifiable facts."

She shook her head and spat again. " 'Tis nobody but yer own dear self this is meant for, m'lord. This be the day foretold by me own abiding spirit as brings sorrow and darkness to you."

I felt a keen prickling of my senses, a tremor in my limbs. "What are you suggesting, madam?"

She was murmuring to herself, her lips writhing, when suddenly she raised her hand before my face. She peered at me between her fingers, moving her hand slightly from side to side. Then, as if satisfied, she dropped it. "Aye, for a certainty, you be the one meant to be part of it."

I sighed. "Part of what?"

She grinned, exposing a maw of missing teeth. Her eyes narrowed, and her countenance bespoke a shrewdish intent. " 'Twill cost ye a tuppence, good sir, but worth it, as you will see. Took me full out of me house to acquaint ye with the calamity as shown to me."

I could not help being interested. "A calamity? Of what sort, Miss Hetta? Is it another barn you see burned, as happens on occasion in these parts, or perhaps some wagonload of hay fallen on the road due to some drunken teamster's negligence? We have printed enough of those stories."

She shook her head angrily. "Rot with yer prattle. A foul deed is shown in my vision." She glanced up at the sun and pointed with her thin arm extended dramatically. "Before yon sun has set this day, mark my words!"

Although unwilling to accept Hetta's glimpse into the future, as I personally had never before been privy to her visions, her assurance disturbed me. "And I am to be part of it, you say?"

"Aye," she said, nodding, her hand extended palm up. "For the rest, I need fair payment, m'lord. A few shillings on me hand, and ye will hear it all."

Torn by curiosity now, I dropped a few pennies into her open palm. "Consider this an advance on more proper payment, Miss Hetta, if your Orphic voice is true. What is it you mean to tell me?"

She thrust the coins into some hidden recess of her voluminous costuming. Then she took a step back, sweeping her arms wide and apart to the heavens, as if she intended to fly immediately. Truly, I was so taken in, I would not have been surprised to see it done.

But she dug her heels into the ground instead, threw her head back, closed her eyes, and her voice rose hoarsely in a runic, singsong chant.

> One from near,
> one from far,
> mischief done
> by morning star.
> The wooded lair
> to doom is wed,
> and damp the hair
> of gold turned red.

I listened attentively, waiting for more revelation than this cryptic verse afforded. She dropped her arms then and turned away.

"Wait, Miss Hetta," I cried. "What does this mean?"

Her pale face twisted toward me. "Death, m'lord."

"But who will it be?" I said. "I don't understand—"

A sudden gust of wind came up, and dust rose from the road

in a thick, blinding cloud. It was of such velocity, stinging my face, that I turned away, shielding my eyes. Within the next moment, the air became less turbulent, the dust storm subsiding. I looked for Hetta, but she was gone.

I saw her then at a far distance, scuttling between the trees. In another moment, she had cut across to the fences and the meadows and woods beyond. I stood rooted, the oddly ominous chant still in my head, making no sense of it. And unaccountably, on this warm morning in July, I shivered.

"Come, Oliver," I told myself, "do not let this persuade you into baseless fear. The woman has always been unsound in her head. Her vision is doubtless as unreliable."

I walked directly then to the newspaper shop of my uncle, albeit more slowly than is my wont. The green of the village square on the old Mill Dam sparkled with its morning dew. I stood there a moment, breathing in the fresh, flowery air, with each breath gaining reassurance. Absently, I jingled the coins in my pocket. A few pennies for a madwoman's fanciful dream. Well worth it, I told myself, smiling now and at ease.

I was unlocking the shop door when I heard loud voices behind me, the sound of scuffling. Looking back, I saw Sam Staples, our deputy sheriff, with Mr. Thoreau in his grasp, leading him into the village jailhouse.

Concerning the Arrest of a Stubborn
Citizen and a Dubious Explanation
of a Prior Misdeed

The Concord jailhouse is a small block building set conveniently in the center of our village. It is behind the main shops on the square and across from our county courthouse. Since there are several taverns along the waterfront, it is helpfully close for our sheriff, Sam Staples, when doing his duty incarcerating the town drunkards and belligerent teamsters who are prone to violent behavior. Because of its central location, any arrest instantly draws a crowd of the morbid and curious.

A motley mob had already gathered as I made my way across, unwilling to breach the door Staples had closed, exchanging their views on what had occurred. Most knew me and gave way as I approached the door, closing in behind in hopes of hearing firsthand the news regarding Mr. Thoreau, whom they considered, in the main, a wastrel and shiftless, no-account sort.

They were still angry with him over a careless fire gone out of control, an event I had covered two years earlier for the *Concord*

Freeman. Then twenty-seven years old, Thoreau had gone fishing with young Edward Hoar, son of the squire, a new student at Harvard. They caught some fish in the Sudbury River, and Thoreau then fried them among the pines at Fair Haven Bay shore. But the wind picked up the fire and carried it along. Out of control, it burned over three hundred acres of the forest. Thereafter, when he passed by, the townspeople and farmers derided him with calls of "Burnt woods!" and "Damned rascal!" which he coldly ignored.

I have known Thoreau since my early childhood but never intimately, as he is thirteen years older and reclusive. Standing at less than normal height, about five feet and seven, he is at once the most narrow-shouldered and thin-chested man I have ever seen. He did not take part in the games and sports at the public school, choosing to be a spectator instead. It was his older brother, John, who was always the more open and agreeable participant. When John died horribly of lockjaw from an infected cut, Thoreau seemed lost. That was two years before the fire, and he became more reclusive than ever.

With his long, slanted nose, large head, and spindly legs, some think him ugly, an unpleasing presence. It is only Louisa May Alcott, second-oldest daughter of Abba and Bronson, who finds him attractive. She has been one of his pupils, and it may be his flighty inclinations to suddenly burst into song, or leap and dance about, that she admires. She is a wild child and equally unpredictable, climbing trees as easily as the boys, nut brown as an Indian, drawing frowns from the villagers for this unseemly, rough behavior, so unlike her more sedate sisters'.

Soon after the fire, I had met Thoreau at Walden Pond to get his explanation for our newspaper. His hut had not yet been built. As we sat together, I became aware of the thick pelt of black hair that covered his arms like a beaver's coat. It was so at odds with the rest of him, which suggested fragility. It was evening, and the scorched woods were still a heavy-scented reminder of the incident. My initial query was about his reaction, and perhaps I put it to him too coldly.

"Do you feel any remorse?" I asked.

He was looking out at the water, his eyes intently following the wind-driven ripples. His attention then shifted to the dark branches of the pines swaying on the opposite side. He inhaled and sighed softly, his head nodding as if in approval of the evening calm. But he did not respond to the question, although I had spoken plainly.

"Mr. Thoreau," I said, as he has always insisted upon a formal address, permitting only Emerson and Bronson Alcott to call him Henry, "surely you must be aware of the questions being asked about this disastrous fire you have admitted to causing by your own negligence. In my uncle's newspaper, we strive for an evenhanded approach to the news, and since you have already been vilified, I am trying to get at your side of it."

His face did not change expression or show any special alertness to my words. His hand found a small stone, and he threw it in a sidearm motion, sending it skimming across the water. Again he nodded at the responsive widening ripples, as if in approval of a natural sequence being demonstrated, but remained stolidly silent. Perhaps, I thought darkly, we shall sit here all night while he counts the ripples and considers them accordingly. He knows me well enough and my business here. Perhaps he is too independent-minded to be concerned about whether he is judged unfairly or not.

Thoreau then shook himself from his reverie and said softly, "Did I feel remorse? Was that your question?"

I nodded, and he then surprised me by drawing several folded sheets of paper from his pocket. "I have been going over the matter in my head, as you might well imagine. It was not as simple a matter to be decided as you suggest, and I have been writing these notes for my journal to clarify my actions for my own mind."

I reached my hand out for the notes, but he shook his head, unfolding them closer to his chest. "You would not have thought, Mr. Puckle, that an errant fire gone out of control would lead to such reasoning as then possessed me. I will take the liberty of reading my thoughts to you."

"Since you have already arrived at a judgment in your mind," I said, "and clarified it in your notes, why not let me have what you have written? I can make a copy of it in my office and return the papers forthwith to you, if you like. There would be no need then to burden yourself with reading it all out to me now while I try to transcribe your words. I should think that would be less a bother for us both." And you can then return to your contemplation of your pond ripples, I thought sourly, wishing to be away from the night wind chilling my neck and this stubborn man, who could not simply admit his fault in allowing hundreds of our forest acres to be carelessly burned down but must talk it over with himself to find some circumstance to assuage his guilt.

Thoreau shook his head. His large, deep-set blue-gray eyes stared into mine, and he then leaned forward, speaking in his fashion with clenched fist.

"No, it would be no bother for my part," he said. "And reading aloud to you what I have written may clarify my mind even more, and I might then arrive at perhaps an even better explanation of the incident and how I perceived its effect. So you may listen and take notes or not, as you like."

I waved my hand passively in agreement and turned up my shirt collar. "Read it then, if you must, and I will try to keep up with you in my own hand."

He nodded briskly, assembled the papers in his hand, and commenced reading. "I had felt like a guilty person, nothing but shame and regret. But now I settled the matter with myself shortly. I said to myself, Who are these men who are said to be the owners of these woods, and how am I related to them?"

I held my hand up to induce his silence while I scribbled to keep pace with him. His words caused me further unease, as I began to sense the curious pathway of his mind, but I had to hear it all now, and nodded for him to go on.

"I have set fire to the forest," he continued, "but I have done no wrong therein."

I quelled my instinct to argue with him and merely nodded as I wrote, sensing the deeper waters ahead.

"I settled it with myself and stood to watch the approaching flames. It was a glorious spectacle, and I was the only one there to enjoy it."

Well, there it is, I told myself as I wrote, no wastrel would have described his feelings better, the man has no civic conscience whatsoever. To set the matter clearly, I said sharply, "Then you do admit your guilt?"

He said, without consulting his notes, "Every creature is better alive than dead, men and moose and pine trees, and he who understands it aright will rather preserve its life than destroy it."

Ha! thought I, some acknowledgment here at last, even-tempered in vagueness as it seems. "Well, that is better, Mr. Thoreau," said I. "That statement may help undo the bad feelings your fire has aroused in our villagers."

He waved his hand, cutting me off impatiently, and resumed his reading aloud. "Strange that so few ever come to the woods to see how the pine lives and grows and spires, lifting its ever-green arms to the light, to see its perfect success, but most are content to behold it in the shape of many broad boards brought to market, and deem *that* its true success."

I held my hand up again to interrupt while I copied his exact words. The man is obviously mad, I thought, letting his thoughts stray to such ends, but perhaps such thinking is excusable considering the outlandish amount of time he spends in these woods; I have never thought ill of a broad board in my life thus far, nor good of it, either, save that it is far better than dirt under my boots.

Thoreau continued to read when my hand came to rest. "But

the pine is no more lumber than man is, and to be made into boards and houses is no more its true and highest use than the truest use of a man is to be cut down and made into manure. There is a higher law affecting our relation to pines as well as to men. A pine cut down, a dead pine, is no more a pine than a dead human carcass is a man."

My pencil was flying across my note papers. It is the most perfect writing tool of our day, designed and manufactured by John Thoreau Senior, ofttimes with Henry's help. The Thoreau pencil's graphite is superior to any other made in America and those imported from Europe. They sell for seven cents each. My uncle buys them at the gross for nine dollars. After years of failure in many different enterprises, it appears that at last the Thoreaus might be self-supporting, a decent reward for the old man, who spends all his hours in the tiny shop behind the house.

I considered Thoreau's last poetic surge of language. While he was grave and serious, as usual, I knew he was capable of daring, flashing wit when least expected, and what he had said to this point might easily be brought down by an opposite sally to his own argument.

"Henry," I said, daring by my familiarity to trigger his temper, as I was becoming increasingly annoyed with his reasoning, "am I to understand that you are equating setting the woods on fire with cutting them down?"

He stared unwaveringly at me. "Is it the lumberman, then, who is the friend and lover of the pine, stands nearest to it, and understands its nature best? Is it the tanner who barked it, or he who has boxed it for turpentine, whom posterity will fable to have been changed into a pine at last? No! No! It is the poet."

I should not have been surprised by his reasoning. He never thought as others, never extolled their way of life, indeed considered every aspect of their days, from politics to religion, to be at odds with genuine freedom, whether of mind or body.

"It is the poet," he repeated firmly. "He it is who makes the truest use of the pine, who does not fondle it with an ax, nor tickle it with a saw, nor stroke it with a plane, who knows whether its heart is false without cutting into it, who has not bought the stumpage of the township on which it stands. All the pines shudder and heave a sigh when that man steps on the forest floor. No, it is the poet who loves them as his own shadow in the air, and lets them stand."

I scribbled as fast as I was able to keep up with his fanciful prose, noting how each phrase could be so true to his relationship with nature and still strange to another such as I, who was unable to share that sensitivity, and I wondered which of us was the crazy one. Then I saw that I had reached the end of my note-taking paper. I showed the full sheaf to him. "One last thought to sum up, that I can carry back in my head. On the pine, if you can state it briefly."

He clenched his fist again, and spoke with undiminished energy. "It is as immortal as I am, and perchance will go to as high a heaven, there to tower above me still."

There came a distant rumble of thunder in the skies. The clouds grew thicker and darker. There was a crackling flash of lightning. It began to rain fiercely. I put my papers away, thanked him, and took to my heels. I heard his laughter and looked back. He sat there, head bared, face uplifted along with his arms, as if happily embracing the storm come suddenly to his Walden Pond.

Since I have heretofore seen no need for an accounting of my days and endeavors, I must profit from that old Thoreau interview, wherein he demonstrated the benefits of testing one's thoughts and reactions to certain events. I knew that Emerson and Bronson Alcott, our most prominent thinkers, kept journals, and that Thoreau was very much under the influence of Emerson, whom he regarded as a kind of literary father figure.

I must include therefore my own conclusion as to what passed between us at Walden Pond. In his elaborate defense of the pines and forest, I sensed the isolation Thoreau felt, his inability to warrant the regard and respect given to Emerson and Alcott, forcing him ever closer to his daily communion with nature. Previously, I had known him as a solitary man given to eccentric attitudes and postures, and only learned more of him by his occasional lectures sponsored by the Lyceum, but in that moment he somehow became more authoritative and purposeful in my eyes. That is why I felt a sudden sympathy when—two years later—I saw him taken into custody, wondering what new transgression he had made against the public good, if it was another accident or perhaps this time a deliberate action to make himself known and taken into account in the village.

Regarding an Interview
in the Jailhouse

Before Sam Staples became Concord's sheriff and jailer, he was a bartender at the hotel across at the Mill Dam, the Middlesex, which burned down last year and was rebuilt. Sheriff Moore was the chief constable then and lived in a house alongside the hotel. Now Staples has his apartment in the jail itself. He is a good-natured man with no pretense. His daughter Ellen lives there with him.

Our town selectmen, who hired Staples, authorized his salary to be the same as that of the local schoolteacher, one hundred dollars a year. As with some teachers, he is also given six cords of firewood as an inducement. This is in keeping with the general dispersal of wages. The Irish laborers who built the railroad worked sixteen hours for their daily pay of fifty cents, and most day laborers received twenty-five cents more for fewer hours. Thoreau receives the same for his carpentry work, and has shoveled manure for seventy-five cents a day. My uncle pays me the same. Staples does not complain of his salary, nor do I. The only two men in Concord who earn more are the ministers of our two churches, who are given five dollars a week for doing God's work.

The jail has walls of solid stone, two or three feet thick. The door of wood and iron is a foot thick. There is iron grating over the windows throughout, straining the light. Some prisoners have escaped their cells by sawing through these grated windows, but no stronger method has yet been installed to prevent these attempts at freedom. Sheriff Staples, bearded and bulky, is accustomed to my visits to his jailhouse in pursuit of news and is not averse to seeing his name in our paper detailing what new miscreant he has arrested.

Upon my arrival, some of the prisoners were milling around the inner corridor stretching their legs. Staples dispersed them by gently saying, "Back to your cells, boys, I've got some business here needs attending." They withdrew at once to their confines without argument, closing their iron-barred doors behind them.

I did not see Thoreau, and Staples grinned at me with twinkling eyes, anticipating my question. "I thought it'd be you, Oliver, knowing you'd seen us across the square. Bit of news scratchin', be it?"

"I'll have more for my story, Sam, when you enlighten me," said I. "Have you arrested Mr. Thoreau, then? If so, on what charge did you bring him here?"

There was a large metal ring of keys in Staples's hand, and he spun it around a moment as he thought about what I had said.

"Well, now, Oliver," he said placatingly, "there can't rightfully be one of what you asked without the other, now can there?"

"Then deal with the first one, if you would. Have you arrested Thoreau?"

"Aye," he said, nodding, "but mind, there was no resistance. Come willingly, he did, when I came across him leaving the cobbler's. Left his shoe for repair there, as luck would have it."

"But what's he done? Why have you arrested him?"

"No secret about that," Staples said. "The man's a scofflaw. The selectmen give me a warrant to arrest him."

"Arrest Thoreau? On what charge?"

Staples turned and stepped across to his desk. He picked up a long sheet of paper, read it briefly, and cast it down. "Nonpayment of his poll tax is the charge. Ain't paid none the past six years, matter of fact. The board of selectmen been proper upset about that, and they left it up to me to work out, which I just did, which you witnessed."

I heard shouting from the back room, where prisoners were kept. I recognized Thoreau's voice, but his words were not clear. The matter still puzzled me, and I returned my attention to the sheriff. "What I fail to understand, Mr. Staples, is why you've neglected the matter for the past six years, as you've admitted, but arrested him today."

Sheriff Staples grinned. "There's a simple answer to that, Oliver. Maybe you don't know it, maybe it ain't no news worthy of your attention, but come next week, my term as deputy sheriff is over. The county will be deciding on the proper man to follow me here."

"What's that to do with it?" I asked in wonder.

He shrugged his bulky shoulders. "They put it to me, the selectmen did, that my books had to be up to date when I left office." Seeing my look of impatience, he continued, rubbing his thick hands together. "They made it clear, y'see, that if Thoreau didn't pay what was due, I would have to make up the proper amount outta me own pocket."

"I see," I said. "Perhaps you can enlighten me on the amount Mr. Thoreau owes on his tax."

"One dollar and fifty cents," Staples said.

"Surely he is able to pay the amount due," I said.

Staples shrugged, raising his hands as if puzzled, too. "Aye, Oliver, able maybe, but he refuses. It's a matter of principle with our Mr. Thoreau, y'see. Has a dim view of taxes, as is well known. But this time, he wants it to be known, it's because of our war with Mexico."

I was aware of our President Tyler annexing Texas last year, and the consequent war with Mexico, which began this May, with Mr. Polk now our president.

"I don't understand, Mr. Staples," I said. "What's the poll tax to do with our war with Mexico?"

Staples wagged his thumb over his shoulder toward the cell in the back room. "Maybe his nibs will explain it. What he told me was, he won't let his dollar buy a man, or a musket to shoot one with."

"Perhaps he is right, then, Mr. Staples, and if more of us followed Mr. Thoreau's stand, our country would not be able so readily to engage in needless war."

"I don't rightly know about that," Staples said. "This here is the poll tax for the state of Massachusetts. It ain't nothin' to do with the war."

"Still," I said, "I recall Bronson Alcott refusing to pay his poll tax several years ago. You did not jail him, did you?"

He wagged his head, grinning again. "Aye, I did not, because Squire Hoar came and paid Alcott's tax for him."

"Mr. Thoreau is a friend of Squire Hoar's as well," I said. "I'm certain that if he is informed, Squire Hoar would be happy to pay this second tax."

Staples now shook his head, his countenance losing its geniality. "Maybe he would, Oliver, but our Mr. Thoreau has made it plain, he has not paid his tax in principle bound, and is not agreeable to anybody paying it for him."

"In that event," I said, "how long will you hold him?"

Staples shrugged and lit up his pipe. "Until I get what is due in hand, Oliver. You want to write a piece about that, it's only fair. The citizens wouldn't want any special favors for our Mr. Thoreau, as you can imagine. You put it to a vote, my guess is they'd want the tax to be paid double."

"Because of the fire in the woods?"

"Aye. He was never proper punished for that, y'know. Burned all them acres of prime wood and never got to be fined for the deed."

"Well, Sam," I said, "I spoke with him about that later. He admitted his guilt. But it was an unforeseen wind that carried the cooking fire away. An unfortunate accident."

Staples waved his evil-smelling pipe, dispelling some of the noxious smoke filling the air, but not enough of it. "An unfortunate accident if it happen to you, Oliver, or maybe some other townsman. But he's the one lives in them woods. He's the one talks to the fish and the birds and most critters there. Talks to the trees, too, I hear.

"Well, it seems to me, that kind of person lives in the woods like he be an Algonquin Injun, he oughta know what can happen with a fire, and wind's a part of that nature he's always ranting about, ain't it? So with him, it can't be no such thing like an accident. He shoulda knowed better."

It was no use my defending Mr. Thoreau any longer with regard to that incident, as unfortunately my thoughts ran parallel with those of Staples. It was not my business to judge Thoreau, but I had found his explanation inexcusable nevertheless. That matter, however, was past and done with, and still at hand was the current issue of his imprisonment.

"Would it be all right, Sam, for me to have a few moments with him? I believe when our villagers read your side of this incident, they will be curious about Thoreau's. I'm not suggesting any advocacy of his resisting proper payment of his tax, merely stating what you have already told me, but in his own words."

Staples thought for a moment, then nodded. "It be fair, Oliver. I never found you writin' lies on how I run my jail to suit your own mind. Go on back and talk to him, if you like. I'll wait here."

The narrow hall leading to the cell was dimly lit, and I could barely discern Mr. Thoreau behind the bars. He was seated on a low stool, his back to the soiled wall, reading from a small pamphlet. To my surprise, I saw another prisoner sharing the same cell. He was stretched out on the floor, dirty and unkempt, mumbling incoherently, his eyes vacant. He reeked of spirits, and I recognized him as our town derelict and drunk, Bert Wheeler.

"Mr. Thoreau," I said, "I'm surprised to find you in such low company. Have you been introduced to Mr. Wheeler?"

Thoreau sniffed, his lips curling. "I've seen his like before. The man has a pernicious habit and was already in his drunken stupor when Sheriff Staples showed me in. Perhaps in a few days, he will recover his wits and become sober enough for us to converse sensibly, exchanging our views on society."

"A few days?" I said. "Then it is true, as Mr. Staples stated, that you do not wish to be released by another's paying your poll tax for you?"

Thoreau put the pamphlet into his coat pocket. "Mr. Puckle," he said, "is that what you are suggesting, that you want to pay the tax for me?"

I shook my head. "I would not dream of any suggestion for your situation, Mr. Thoreau, inasmuch as your own views are best suited to the conduct of your life. I am asking merely for any explanation of the charge against you, in order that I may write about it in our paper, without injury to you. I take it that Mr. Staples has incarcerated you for nonpayment of poll tax. Is that the case?"

He nodded. "A wise man will not leave the right to the mercy of chance, nor wish it to prevail through the power of the majority."

"You are encouraging civil disobedience, then?"

"I was not born to be forced," he said. "I will breathe after my own fashion. If a plant cannot live according to its nature, it dies; and so a man."

I was busy writing down his exact words. "Mr. Staples said your main objection to the tax involved our war with Mexico. Is that true?"

"When a sixth of the population of a nation which has undertaken to be the refuge of liberty are slaves, and a whole country is unjustly overrun and conquered by a foreign army, and subjected to military law, I think that it is not too soon for honest men to rebel and revolutionize."

"I understand, Mr. Thoreau," I said, "but according to what Mr. Staples has explained to me, since you are against your dollar being used to buy a musket to wage a war, you are in your own fashion declaring war against the state."

"Yes," he said.

"Then you are of the opinion," I said, "that it is just to disregard what others consider to be the law?"

"Mr. Puckle," he answered, rising and stepping closer to me, his large eyes luminous in the dimly lit cell, "if the injustice is of such nature that it requires you to be the agent of injustice to another human being, then I say, break the law."

I completed my note taking and put the paper in my coat pocket. "Very well, Mr. Thoreau, and thank you for your comments. I will have them printed in our newspaper. And good day to you, sir."

As I was turning away, he said, "Blessed are they who never

read a newspaper, for they shall see Nature, and, through her, God."

Staples was sitting at his desk, puffing strongly on his pipe, when I returned. "Well," he said, "did he explain his dislike for paying his tax, Oliver?"

"Indeed," I said. "He doesn't think much of newspapers, either."

About the Fair Visitor from Boston in Search of a Situation

My uncle had taken the early stage to Boston, on a business trip to purchase new typefaces available now in their newspapers and in the New York City press. I had urged him to take the train instead, as the ride would certainly have been more comfortable. The train fare is only fifty cents to Boston, whereas the stagecoach costs one dollar more. Further, the train takes only one hour to the stage's four. But he was resistant to my logic.

"We've only had the railroad the past two years, Oliver," he said. "How do I know the fool thing won't break down and upset my scheduled time of arrival? The stage is the longer way, no doubt, but it has never failed me yet, nor do I expect it will this morning. I'll take my chances with horses over mechanical contraptions any day."

After he left, I prepared the news copy for the compositor and pressman in the shop behind the office. It was time then to review my interview notes regarding Thoreau and Staples. Sheriff Staples had not mentioned the fact, but according to Massachusetts law, he did have an alternative to jailing Thoreau. The condition is always that property of the person charged can be confiscated instead. Staples had simply gone to the heart of the matter, knowing Thoreau had nothing worth confiscating, and taken the next available step, of confinement. The only property Thoreau has is the tiny hut he built last year on land belonging to Emerson. Simply furnished, it contains little to compensate a debt-hungry state. It is ten feet wide by fifteen feet long, with a garret and closet, a large window at each side, and two trapdoors. The brick fireplace is opposite the door. The cellar is used for storing beans and potatoes, which Thoreau grows, along with corn, peas, and turnips.

How Thoreau came to have the hut may be of interest. His friend Emerson bought up much of the land around Walden Pond, which is a lovely lake not quite two miles from Concord village. Emerson told Thoreau that if he would clear the scrubland there and reforest it with pines, he was free to build a cabin on the property and stay without paying rent. Thoreau himself had surveyed the lake and found it to be half a mile long and a third of a mile wide. He determined to earn his living as a writer, and the cabin, he thought, would eliminate his need to make money while he lived cheaply off the land.

As this was Thoreau's only seizable property, I concluded that Sheriff Staples had done the best he could with an improvident tax evader, notwithstanding his prisoner's specious reasoning. I took pains to transcribe his exact words, worrying meanwhile that my uncle would not look with favor on my granting free use of our space to such verbosity.

Reflecting upon this, and on the verge of trying to cut some phrases out and reword others, I was startled by the sudden opening of our front door, and the appearance of a stranger. I rose in confusion and stood transfixed as a maiden of the loveliest countenance, superbly dressed, turned from the door with exquisite grace to face me.

Her eyes were the clearest blue and utterly without guile. Her nose was delicately formed, her smile radiant. Golden hair as soft and fine as silk framed her noble brow, and upon it, provocatively tilted, rested a tawny Tuscan hat. She wore a brown satin frock with pearl buttons, a blue scarf about her slender neck, and in her white-gloved hand was a light-colored parasol, the same hue as her shoes. Truly, I had never before beheld any as lovely. If she had not spoken first, I might have remained dumbstruck, staring at this vision forever.

Her eyes shifted past mine and focused on the wall to the side of my desk. "How quaint," she said, her lips parting in a curving smile.

"What?" I asked, turning to see what had got her notice. Immediately I groaned, embarrassed beyond belief. It was a small white card that years earlier Uncle Rufus had put up.

She was reading from it, her voice light and merry. " 'Avoid alluring company.' However did you come by that admonition?"

I plucked it off the wall, willing to destroy it. "It is a maxim of Mr. Webster's," I said lamely. "He had a host of similar cautions in our spelling books. This is my uncle's newspaper. He has reared me, and placed the constraint, I suppose, to ensure my constant devotion to my work here."

She touched her fingertips to her lips in an apparent attempt to stifle her laughter, but it bubbled through nevertheless. "I would not have thought," she said, "that in this small village, there were that many temptations to ensnare you."

"There well may be," I said lamely, "but in truth, if they so abound, I know them not. My work is the consuming interest of my hours, and I have little time to consider what might perhaps be more pleasurable and rewarding."

"But surely," she said, "your work cannot be of such overriding importance as to be your sole interest in life?"

"Sadly, dear lady, I must confess that it is, and has been, my total focus. My uncle is old and dependent upon me, as he has no other to discharge such reportorial skills as I may possess. But even if that were not so, I admit that I have never chafed at the duties I am obliged to contribute, and have found the utmost satisfaction in discharging them as best I can."

She then threw up her hands as if in mock surrender. "Well, then," she said, "perhaps you have found the secret of life, to be so centered. I am truly sorry I mocked you."

I shook my head, not satisfied with my explanation. "No need to apologize, as I do not take it so. To explain further, it is a habit I have become accustomed to, and there may be something that can be said against this 'centering,' as you describe it. I have simply known nothing better."

She reached out her hand as if to touch mine but withdrew it, making a face that expressed a certain wry acceptance. "Surely it is no business of mine to cause you any doubts. If the card has directed you, and saved you thus far, please replace it as it was, and continue to draw moral strength from its injunction. It would be on my head forever if, to please me, you were persuaded to fall from grace, and descend into iniquity."

Without thought now, and sensing my face had turned red in my discomfiture, I tore the card into several pieces and tossed them upon my desk. Her mouth opened in dismay at my action, but she said nothing. "I should have done that years ago, when he first placed it there. But I have lived here in Concord all my life, and there was never reason before to question those words. I simply accepted them as a maxim. Indeed, I am grateful for your calling it to my attention, as I have had it before my eyes for so long that in truth the words no longer carry any meaning."

She was nodding, smiling again. "Yes, I can see that one can become so used to a thing that one no longer knows it is there. Perhaps it is time for your uncle to provide a new card that will engage your attention."

At ease now, I shook my head. "You are the one who has done that. Now that you are here, how may I help you?"

"Does your newspaper include a classified page that lists employment opportunities?" she asked.

"Indeed it does," I replied. The latest issue was on my desk, and I reached for it, showing her the back inside page.

She studied the columns for a moment. "Does your paper have a wide circulation here?"

"Not as much as my uncle Rufus would like, but inasmuch as we are the only source of news in Concord, one might say it is read by a goodly number of our local residents. What do you have in mind?"

"I should like to insert a line to this effect: Respectable young lady seeks situation."

"Is this for yourself?" I asked.

"Certainly. Why else would I be here?"

"I could not have guessed, madam—"

"Miss," she said.

"So much the better," I said. "But you are not yourself a resident of Concord?"

Her voice was firm. "Indeed not. I've just come from Boston, having left my previous employer, and intend to take residence here and find another position."

I wrote the line she requested and studied it in silence. There were many questions I wanted to ask, but I was unable to frame them without possible offense.

Impatient with my studied manner, she asked, "Is there anything wrong, Mr.—?"

"Oliver Puckle. And you are—?"

"Margaret Roberts. You are frowning as if disturbed. May I inquire as to the reason?"

"To begin with, you do not specify what type of position you are seeking, nor indeed what it is you do best. I would have imagined your specifying a particular situation with which you find yourself agreeable. The line, if inserted just as you requested, would be interpreted most generally, and the response you might get would be in any category, and thus fitting you with a suitable prospective employer would be a matter of luck."

Her eyes gleamed, and she smiled, her head arching back gracefully. "Yes, Mr. Puckle, that is exactly what I have in mind. I have left Boston for good, come to Concord with an open mind, and will let my chance for luck decide." She was opening her bag, her hand stirring inside. "What is the charge, sir?"

I put up my hands, waving away her proffered coins. "If it be luck to keep you here," I said grandly, "may I start you off in that direction. We will be happy to insert the line you require without charge, Miss Roberts."

She stared at me, her lips parted in surprise. "It is most kind of you, Mr. Puckle, but do you speak for your uncle, who may not be as generous?"

"Uncle has gone to Boston this day," I said, smiling, "and if he questions my sponsoring you, I can obtain the advertisement at a lower price."

"Well, I do thank you," she said. "It is most agreeable to arrive at a new place and find a stranger so generous."

"It is my pleasure," I said, still giddy at the sight of her. "Perhaps in due time we will meet again, and I will not be such a stranger. Where will you be staying?"

She bit her lip, and her eyes opened wider. "Why, as yet, I have no idea. I came here directly from the train. Perhaps you can suggest someplace suitable, and not too expensive."

"There is the Middlesex Hotel, but I doubt you would find it inexpensive." Casting about wildly in my mind, anxious to ensure her safety and well-being, I suddenly thought of the most desirable. "There is the Thoreau house."

"Do you think I would find that congenial?"

"Most congenial," I said firmly. "Mr. Thoreau, the younger, that is, has a reputation as a poet. You may have heard of him?"

She shook her head. "Regrettably, Mr. Puckle, I have not. I do not read much poetry, as I find it too fanciful."

"No matter," I said. "His reputation is minor thus far, and no doubt has not extended to your city. But his mother does take in boarders. There are several aunts there, and his sisters, all of the highest intelligence and grace, and I am certain they would find your presence equally attractive. There are others in Concord where you might find lodging, but I have known the Thoreau family all my life, and cannot speak too highly of their custom and civility."

"You make them sound quite attractive indeed, Mr. Puckle. But remember, please, I am interested in finding reasonable lodging as well."

"I am quite familiar with their charges, Miss Roberts. Mrs. Thoreau will provide a pleasant room with light for seventy-five cents a week. Is that within your means?"

She did not hesitate with calculations. "Why, yes, well within, and perhaps after I secure some employment, I will be able to afford better."

"You will find none better in Concord village," I said. "Mrs. Thoreau is a good cook and perhaps an even better conversationalist. Her two daughters are near your age and both gentle and friendly. There are also some new ladies staying there, and they are all of the same mold, cultured and reasonable, and they would welcome you as part of the family."

Her face had brightened with each word of assurance from

my lips. "Very well, Mr. Puckle, you have convinced me. Now if you would be so kind as to direct me there."

I walked to the door and opened it. "Walk back down our Main Street the way you came from the railroad station, cross the tracks, and it will be the second house on your right. If you would care to mention that I have recommended you there, you will be afforded a room with no further ado."

"Thank you again, Mr. Puckle, you have been most kind," she said, moving out the door. "No doubt we shall see each other again."

"I will pray for that chance, Miss Roberts," I said, inhaling her fragrance as she passed. Then pointing, I said, "Have you no baggage?"

"It was left at the station, Mr. Puckle," she said. "I shall arrange to have it picked up after your Mrs. Thoreau has confirmed my lodging. Good morning to you."

She walked away with an assured grace, her head moving side to side as she took in the various shops along the square. I watched until she disappeared from view, scarcely able to contain my excitement.

Then, closing the door, I returned to my desk. The torn pieces of the telltale card my uncle had provided for my continuing welfare lay where I had cast them. In a moment of whimsy, I rearranged them again to fit their original form. AVOID ALLURING COMPANY. I looked down at the black letters for a long moment, then, laughing, I swept them into the waste basket. With a light heart, I then read again the few words I had scribbled for our classified column: "Respectable young lady seeks situation."

It had troubled me when first she spoke those words. Questions were rising within me now, one after another, that I was unable to still. Why had she come? Why leave Boston for the smaller, less exciting village of Concord? What sort of position had she held there? What sort would she find available here? And finally, most insistent of all, how soon would I be able to see her again?

The Spirited Louisa May Alcott
and Her Intuition

At the noon hour, I had made much progress in the composition of the copy for my uncle to edit upon his return and decided to have my lunch. My aunt Martha always provides a few sandwiches for me, along with an apple. The scent of her bread, freshly baked every day, was so tantalizing, my fingers ripped the paper apart with uncommon viciousness. I was scarcely two bites into the thick, cold roast beef when the front door of the shop opened.

My young friend Louisa Alcott had her head only in the opening. "Are you busy, Mr. Puckle?"

"Never too busy for you, Louisa May," I said. "Do come in. You are just in time for lunch."

The rest of her appeared, a coltish girl with bright brown eyes and an exuberant nature. "Oh, I've already had my lunch, Mr. Puckle," she said. "But if you don't mind, I'll just sit and keep you company."

It is common knowledge that her father, Bronson, though highly regarded as a prophet and fiery speaker, has never made enough money to support his wife, Abba, and their four girls. They are all like skeletons. To make matters worse, since Bronson weaves, designs, and cuts their linen garments, their dresses look like cut-down bedsheets. They go without shoes, barefoot in all weather, and have little more than prayer and water at breakfast. Sometimes there might be a turnip or potato.

I pushed one sandwich closer to my guest. "Please join me, Louisa. I find it awkward to eat alone with another watching."

She looked at me suspiciously. "Are you sure? It doesn't disturb me in the least."

"Indeed?" I said. "Well then, humor me, as two of these would be too much and might put me to sleep."

"If you insist," she said. Her dark, soiled hand darted out, crammed the sandwich into her mouth, and it was gone.

I rolled the apple to her. "Have this, too. It will keep you occupied, while I finish mine."

She perched herself upon my desk, arranged her floppy, tentlike dress over her bare brown legs, and bit ravenously into the fruit. I was beginning to regret taking the first sandwich myself, as the child was plainly starving. She finished off the apple and tossed the core into my waste basket.

"I saw your uncle get on the stage this morning," she said. "Where was he going?"

"To Boston, a business trip."

"I hate Boston," she said with bitterness.

"Why?" I asked. "It is a lovely city."

"Oh, you mean the buildings," she said sharply, "the great houses. The people are not so lovely."

I looked at her, remembering now the Alcotts had come to Concord from there six years ago. "Why do you say that?"

"They didn't approve of Father's teaching methods at his school," she said. "They made up a mob outside the door and threatened him for having a little black girl there. They didn't want any niggers, they said. Father insisted she was God's child, as good as any other color. So they made him leave the school, and we left Boston." She rocked back, holding her knees. "They don't like the niggers here any better," she said, her dark eyes smoldering.

"I'm sorry you had that experience, Louisa," I said. "But not everybody here dislikes them. I do not, nor does Mr. Thoreau."

"Yes, I know," she said. "But my father thinks it strange that he alone of his family is not an Abolitionist, joining with us against slavery."

"Louisa," I said, "it is not for us to judge Mr. Thoreau. He may very well be one in principle and yet not admit the fact. For your information, he is, at present, across the street in our jail for demonstrating his own personal convictions."

Her eyes lost their intensity and flew wider. "But whatever for?"

"Refusal to pay his poll taxes."

"Oh, that," she said lightly. "My father will not, either. He would choose to go to jail himself rather than pay."

I laughed. "So Mr. Staples has informed me. Now what really

brings you here today? Are you still trying to sell some of your poems to the *Concord Freeman*?"

She hunched her shoulders and grinned. "Well, yes, Mr. Puckle. I must make some money. I'm nearly fourteen. But that's not the only reason."

I leaned back in my chair, smiling. "Very well. The other reason first, and then I'll read the poems."

"I saw who came in earlier today, with the gold hair, pretty hat, and parasol. Is she to be your wife, Mr. Puckle?"

I stared at her openmouthed. "My wife? What ever gave you that notion?"

She shrugged. "She was so beautiful. It seemed to me you two would look well together."

I patted her hand. "Louisa, I grant you she was indeed beautiful. But I had never seen her before. She had business to do here and came directly from the train." Louisa sat with intense concentration. "From your Boston," I added.

"What kind of business? Is your uncle hiring her to report on the Ladies Antislavery Society?"

"Not to my knowledge. If you must know, she is looking for employment here and wanted to insert a notice in our situations wanted column. That is all I know about her."

Louisa shook her head, her long brown hair, unruly at best, flying across her face. "That is very strange. Does she have friends or relatives here?"

"She did not say."

"Then where will she stay while waiting for her situation to be offered? I'm curious, Mr. Puckle, Oliver, because I may need to do the same myself someday to earn money."

"I referred her to Mrs. Thoreau for lodging. The rate for boarders is most reasonable, and she will find congenial company."

Louisa laughed. "Well, yes, except that Aunt Jane is quite deaf, and Mrs. Thoreau talks on and on without stop."

"True," I said, "but I was thinking more of Helen and Sophia, Henry's sisters, for her companionship."

"Yes, they are nice, but how long can she afford to live there without employment? What kind of position is she seeking?"

"She didn't say, Louisa. I admit I was curious, too. Miss Roberts said it would depend on her luck, implying she would accept whatever came her way."

"Is that her name?"

"The one she gave me. Margaret Roberts."

Louisa stared and cocked her head. "Do you mean it may not be her true name, that she gave you one not her own?"

I shrugged. "She has come to Concord in search of a new life, she told me. It is possible she might like a new name as well."

She sat thinking, rubbing at one of her bare toes. "Like a mystery woman, Mr. Puckle, Oliver—must I call you Mister?"

"I never implied that you should. I call you Louisa."

She exhaled a great rush of air, puffing her cheeks. "Oh, thank you, Mr. Puckle—Oliver, you have no idea how much I hate being formal with you. You're my only grown-up friend."

"Well, Mr. Thoreau is your friend, is he not?"

She nodded, ducking her head. "Yes, but I think that is because he is friends with my father and Mr. Emerson, and they are all transcendentalists. I prefer you, because you are not."

"You don't approve of their theories?"

She looked away. "As my mother says, fine speeches do not put food on the table."

"Have faith, Louisa. Perhaps someday soon your father will be awarded his due and earn a decent living. And in the meantime, if you are so eager to make money, I suggest you give up writing poetry, at which you are assured of starving, and write books instead."

"Books?" she repeated. "Me?"

"Have you read Dickens, or Cooper? They write wonderful books. Or have you read stories by Edgar Allan Poe, or the tales of our own Nathaniel Hawthorne? What do you read?"

"My father gave me the Bible and *Pilgrim's Progress*. Mr. Emerson has invited me to choose from his library. But I don't like Goethe, or Carlyle, or Seneca, or Cicero."

I shook my head. "No, those are not fun for young people to read. There are new books, without pretense of vast knowledge. I shall bring you some of my own from home, Louisa. Books about real people, the joys of their lives, and sometimes the sadder times. It would be a great loss were you not to find your own way of expression."

"Do you really think so, Oliver?" she asked.

"I would not say so if I did not." I held out my hand. "Now I am ready for the poems you wanted to show me."

She surprised me by jumping off the desk and shaking her head. "No, I think not, Oliver. I want to make money for my mother and sisters. If you say poetry is not the answer, I will think about the books."

"Come by tomorrow then," I said. "I promise you will like Charles Dickens. And the very exciting *Robinson Crusoe*."

She was ready to leave but stood at my desk, staring and fingering her lip. "I like your new lady, Margaret Roberts."

My head rolled back in surprise. "Why do you say that?"

Her hand flicked to the empty wall. "She must have encouraged you to remove that silly card you had there."

"You are quite wrong, Louisa. It was my own idea."

She shook her head and patted my shoulder as she stepped toward the door. "Poor Oliver. Now he's at the mercy of everybody."

Concerning the Confusion
Caused by Women

The telegraph wires, whose humming Thoreau admittedly thrilled to, brought me news later that afternoon. The telegram from my uncle Rufus was brief. He believed he would find a better price for what he sought in New York City than in Boston and would proceed there. In the event of his further delay, I was to put together the *Concord Freeman* myself, and see to it that it was published on schedule. In short, I was to be reporter, editor, publisher, and proofreader until his return. Needless to say, I was thrilled and wished my uncle further delay so that I might assume complete control of his newspaper and earn his praise.

I worked at a fury until six o'clock, when I threw my pencil and shears down, and sat back for a moment's ease. I allowed my thoughts to idle, contemplating the day, and what would be necessary for the next. The pencil was again in my hand before I realized it, and as I glanced down at the paper beneath it, I noticed with a start that, however unintentionally, I was writing a name repeatedly, one that had somehow bored into my subconscious and was now making itself known.

Margaret, I had written. Then, *Margaret Roberts*. Then, in consternation, I saw it had become *Margaret Roberts Puckle*, and finally *Mrs. Margaret Puckle!* The demon that always glowed in Louisa Alcott's dark eyes had somehow taken hold of me with her opening question. *Is she to be your wife, Mr. Puckle?* Then a moment later, *It seemed to me you two would look well together.*

Despite my immediate denial, I could not deceive myself. In truth, I had been so shattered by her beauty, it was a wonder that I had managed a single sensible word during our entire conversation.

Again I considered the story Miss Roberts had given me, and once more, I could not believe it in its entirety. I was unable to think of any respectable young lady, supposedly dissatisfied with her life and position in a large city such as Boston, suddenly picking herself up and moving away, without friends or relations, or the far more important aspect, promise of employment. She intended to trust her luck, so she had said, and that, too, seemed a most unlikely basis on which to chance her life.

If her story indeed were true, then we would, of a certainty, meet again. If I were laggard, she would have to come to the paper herself, inquiring of any response to her few words in our classifieds. I thought, too, that since I had been living in Concord all my life, I could assuredly ask among the many shopkeepers I knew so well if they were in need of a salesperson, one of such outstanding beauty and cultured voice and manner that their business would be improved at least a thousandfold were they to hire her. I could get her an interview with anybody of importance. Indeed, knowing of my relationship with Uncle Rufus, the shopkeepers would extend themselves on her behalf to curry favor with Concord's only news publisher. I could show her the villages, the countryside, the rivers. I could take her boating, berry picking, hiking the trails just beyond the edge of the village. We could go swimming, skating in the winter . . .

Such were the wild fancies whirling in my head, and since I could endure no longer this idle speculation riddled with romantic notion, I threw down my pencil, determined of a sudden to see her forthwith, at whatever cost to my pride.

In another moment, I had found my coat and closed the shop. It was early twilight, and across the square, Sam Staples's jail was gray and quiet. Turning my head to the right, I saw the Middlesex Hotel and was instantly overjoyed. I had now found a reasonable pretext on which she could not protest my seeing her again. I would ask her to dinner there, and I hurried now, in fear that Mrs. Cynthia Dunbar Thoreau was already enticing Miss Roberts with an early guest meal.

The morning crowd that had clustered around the jailhouse had gone. If Henry Thoreau was still inside, a prisoner to his convictions, nobody was around outside attesting to that fact. I wondered if I would be the first to bring the news about him to his mother, shortly.

Comprising the Details of
an Unfortunate Visit, with Subsequent
Theories Only to Be Surmised

The Thoreau house is always full of women, spinsters all. They are mostly the aunts of either side of the family, along with other ladies who visit and stay. There is Aunt Maria, the sister of Henry's father, an ardent and articulate member of the Ladies Antislavery Society. There is Aunt Louisa Dunbar, Cynthia Dunbar Thoreau's sister, there since 1830, the only truly religious one of the family. It is said of her that Daniel Webster had taken to her when she was young and a flirt, and had persuaded her to the church. There is Aunt Jane, the near deaf aunt, who went over to Trinitarianism. There are Henry's sisters: Helen, who gives music lessons, and Sophia, the youngest, who paints flowers. There is Mrs. Ward, a widow, and her daughter, Prudence, friends of Aunt Maria since Boston.

Finally, there is Henry's mother, Cynthia, who opened her house and heart to all the relatives, and accepts boarders and lodgers as well, welcoming to her table even visitors who are not staying at her house. She is bright and animated, and, as Louisa Alcott says, given to nonstop talk. Behind the house is the workshop of Henry's father, who was encouraged to go into the pencil business by a neighbor after a series of failures in everything he had turned to. It is believed that John Thoreau Senior is slightly deaf, but it is agreed by common consent that this is a blessing, when one weighs the constant stream of words ever-issuing from the mouth of his wife, and a man's need for peace and quiet.

While Henry Thoreau may revel in nature, he apparently sees no joy in maintaining his family's front lawn, and it has become scrubby and overgrown. There are weeds and crabgrass growing robustly without interference, and the front door needs painting. I hoped Margaret Roberts had not allowed these minor blights to deflect her from her course, to seek proper lodging with Mrs. Thoreau.

It was Henry's mother who answered the door. Behind her stood the elderly aunts Maria and Jane. I peered anxiously past their heads into the darkened front rooms, hoping for a glimpse of Margaret Roberts, but I could not see her among other familiar faces. Mrs. Thoreau greeted me with her customary wide smile and warmth.

"Why, Oliver Puckle, how good of you to call. We have all been waiting for your report."

Taken aback, I could only stammer, in confusion, "Report?"

Aunt Jane, the deaf one, pushed forward. "What's he saying, Cynthia?"

"He hasn't said anything yet, Jane," Mrs. Thoreau said.

"What?" said Aunt Jane.

Mrs. Thoreau, no novice at dealing with the handicapped in hearing, ignored her and addressed me again. "About what happened with Henry this morning, Oliver. Some boys came by and said something about his being involved in a scuffle with Mr. Staples. They couldn't say more but added that you would know more about it, having gone inside the jailhouse to talk to Mr. Staples and Henry."

The aunts had pressed closer now, forming a solid mass at the door, and I could see nothing beyond them. It was obvious to me that before any discussion about Miss Roberts, I had to first settle this matter of their concern about Henry.

"I'm sorry to say, Mrs. Thoreau, that Mr. Staples has found Henry in defiance of the law, for reasons of not paying his poll tax, and has consequently imprisoned him until the amount due is forthcoming."

The ladies did not swoon or recoil in anguish or dismay at this news, as they were probably already conditioned to their darling boy's continuing stand against society and its cherished beliefs, not even the church being excused from his diatribes.

"It's not for me to advise Henry on how to conduct his life," Mrs. Thoreau said. "But I am sure he would prefer playing his flute or wandering in the woods, since he is such a strong advocate of personal freedom. Do you know how much money Mr. Staples requires for us to arrange bail?"

"Mr. Staples is interested only in the exact payment of what is due, ladies," I said, "as otherwise it has to be made up by him, which is against his own principles. For the sum of one dollar and fifty cents, he will give your Henry his freedom."

There was an immediate interchange among the ladies, the poor deaf Aunt Jane being stonily refused an instant translation of what I had said, while Henry's mother was asking who among them had the money needed, as she had none on hand. It was Aunt Maria who then stepped forward, saying, "Squire Hoar always takes care of this for Bronson. Surely he will do as much for our Henry."

"Will you go then, Maria?" Mrs. Thoreau asked. "I have to finish dinner."

The shy daughter of Mrs. Ward, Prudence, a botanist and flower painter, then moved forward. "Is it money for Henry?" she asked. "I believe I have some. Let me look."

With the exception of Mrs. Cynthia Dunbar Thoreau, the ladies turned back into the dark sitting room, all of a clamor. Thoreau's mother said to me, "I really don't understand why Henry must distance himself from everybody on everything, Oliver. I pay my poll taxes, why not he?"

It was a question I was not prepared to answer, and I was saved by the return of the ladies, each with her own pocketbook, rummaging inside for coins. There was a whoop as Prudence's hand emerged with some pennies, then another as her mother showed more. Aunt Jane, sensing now that a simple game requiring money was transpiring, opened her own purse and showed a fistful of silver, copper, and gold currency.

Ignoring the applause of the others, she came directly to me, saying in her strident, rasping voice, "Here you are, Oliver. I don't know what this is about, but perhaps somebody will explain the matter to me soon."

I held up my hands and backed off a step. Aunt Maria reached over, took Aunt Jane's hand, and emptied it into her own. "Thank you, Jane. I'll take this up to Mr. Staples now."

"Why am I giving money to Mr. Staples?" Aunt Jane asked.

Aunt Maria patted her arm. "Cynthia will explain."

She looked at me, then over my head at the darkening sky. "Do you know, Oliver, at what time Mr. Staples closes his office?"

I shrugged. "It varies, Aunt Maria, depending upon what urgency of business keeps him there past his supper."

"I will hurry, then," she said, bustling past me. "I cannot endure the thought of Henry spending his night in jail."

She went down the walk at a brisk clip for her age. "I'll save dinner, Maria," Mrs. Thoreau called. The other ladies were retreating to the front parlor. Henry's mother took a step back and was offering her hand. "Thank you so much for taking the trouble, Oliver. Do call again."

She seemed intent on closing her door then, and I was suddenly galvanized into remembering my original reason for being there. "About Miss Roberts," I said, "did you provide a room for her, and do you not think her attractive?"

Her eyes looked into mine blankly. "What Miss Roberts? Who is she?"

"Why, the young lady who asked me this morning about lodging. I sent her directly to you."

She wagged her head. "If you did, perhaps she lost her way, Oliver. No Miss Roberts has come here. There have been no visitors at all."

"But I watched her progress, Mrs. Thoreau. She was planning to come straight to you when she left me this morning."

"Well then, she must have changed her mind and gone to try lodging elsewhere," she said. "The lawn is unkempt, as you can plainly see, and perhaps she thought such neglect indicative of the interior. I would not blame your young lady, Oliver. I have already spoken to Henry about it too many times."

I was truly stunned. "You are certain to have been here at home since this morning, then?"

"Yes, Oliver, most certainly. I am sorry to disappoint you. Do call again when Henry returns. He will wish to express his own thanks for your trouble."

Wherein the Narrator
Conducts a Search to No Account

There are many houses in our village like Mrs. Thoreau's for permanent lodgers or overnight travelers. In the dim light of evening, I hastened from one to another, struggling with my memory when no bed-and-breakfast sign showed. To all my inquiries, I received the same negative response. There was no Miss Roberts recently arrived in Concord, nor indeed any young lady answering to her description. Finally I had reached the south end of the village, where the road forks into open country. There were no more houses for me to look into here, and I had to turn back. I could not imagine what might have befallen Miss Roberts. There was a possibility that she might have turned back toward the center square, perhaps choosing the Middlesex Hotel for its overall good qualities and disregarding the cost. With racing heart, I hastened there.

The street was quiet in the enveloping darkness, the great elms along Main Street casting huge shadows on the ground. I had nearly reached the square when I was greeted by a loud "Halloo!" from a shadowy figure bustling toward me. It was Aunt Maria on her return journey.

"Well, Oliver," she said, "how very nice to see you again."

"It is good to see you, too, Aunt Maria," I said. "How did it go with Mr. Staples, then?"

"You may be interested to know," she said, "that I have made the required arrears payment in full, just as you indicated was necessary."

I looked past her but could see nothing else in the night. "Then where is Henry?" I asked.

"Henry is quite well," she said.

"I don't understand," I said. "You paid the amount due, you said?"

"That is indeed a matter to be gone into," she said, "and one which I do not understand, either. Mr. Staples, it appears, has gone for his supper. His daughter Ellen was there in his stead. It was Ellen to whom I gave the money for Henry's release."

Again I asked, "Then where is Henry?"

Aunt Maria stood striving for calm, making a face. "The girl accepted payment, made a note to that effect, then told me she did not have access to the cell key. It was not for her to release prisoners, but her father."

"Well, then, where was Mr. Staples?"

Aunt Maria shrugged her ample shoulders. "He was there but unavailable to perform that duty." She hesitated. "The reason she gave was clearly preposterous."

"That being?" I prodded.

"He had retired to his apartment and removed his boots. Ellen said he is loath then to put them on again. Therefore, Henry will spend the night in jail, since Mr. Staples is not available due to his reluctance to appear in bare feet."

"I'm sorry, Aunt Maria," I said. "Did you by chance speak to Henry?"

She puffed her cheeks in exasperation. "Well, you know him well enough. Was he grateful? Did he applaud his aunt for taking the trouble to raise the money on his behalf, then hiking through the night to rescue him? Indeed not! Rather, he was furious at me for interfering in his rights, he said, and how else would Concord awake to its tyranny?"

I smiled and patted her hand in attempted comfort, as she has always been a kind soul, most indulgent to me in my childhood, and is, indeed, like a very dear aunt to me.

"I'm sorry, Aunt Maria," I said. "He said nearly the same to me, and at far greater length, as is his custom. However, if Mr. Staples chooses not to act tonight, as is likely, I am confident he will release Henry first thing tomorrow morning, when he will have his boots on, and a better face of his responsibilities."

We bid each other a good night then, and she hurried back to the Thoreau house, taking great strides in her unmistakable gait. I watched until the darkness had settled so I could see her no longer and then, taking a quick breath, resumed my own unhappy errand.

There are three additional lodging houses at the north end of the village, where I was now, close to Uncle Rufus's home, but Miss Roberts had not appeared at them, either. I saved the hotel for last and questioned the proprietor of a roadside tavern that at times took transients. The owner shook his head; he had taken in no newcomers this day. There were patrons in the side stalls and on the barstools, and he suggested that my lady might be there on the premises. I thought not but looked nevertheless. He suggested then that I try the Middlesex, and I shook his hand and agreed it was a chance worth the taking, and that it would be my next destination.

The proprietor of the hotel is Barnaby Fields. He has known me from birth, gave me the name Oliver after much debate with my uncle, his closest friend, and has been godfather, uncle, and surrogate father as well. I have chopped his firewood for as long as I can remember, and helped in the hotel kitchen during summer tourist seasons when my uncle Rufus had not yet found use for me on his newspaper. Barnaby's wife died at an early age, leaving him bereaved, and it took years before he regained his sunny disposition. His principles are as firm as those of my uncle Rufus, but he finds more pleasure in life. He is as fond of Spanish port as of his after-dinner cigar, and is now without question the most cheerful and popular man in Concord.

As I entered his hotel, he bounced across the floor to embrace me warmly. "Well, Oliver, my boy, it is good to see you. Have you decided to forgo Martha's kidney pie tonight and to chance our lamb stew instead?"

"No, Uncle Barnaby," I said. "I am here on another matter, of extreme urgency and concern to me."

He drew back a step to appraise my face. "Well, good heavens, what is it, lad? You look as if taken by the plague."

"That could not trouble me more," I said. "I am looking for a person who seems to have quite disappeared. To your knowledge, Uncle, has a Miss Roberts registered for a room at your hotel?" He stared, and I added, "She is from Boston."

"Miss Roberts? What is her full name, Oliver, and is she traveling alone?"

"Margaret Roberts. Alone, yes, I believe. She came directly to our newspaper this morning, without luggage, saying she had left it at the station."

He went behind the high counter, found the register book, and turned it toward me, so I could read the page with him. "I see none by that name, Oliver. From Boston, you said. There is the elderly gentleman, Falwell, from Cambridge. The sisters from Philadelphia, the Jordans. The wine salesman from Providence, Sutter. That is all thus far today. Perhaps she will drop by later."

I shook my head, at a loss as to where to look next.

He pushed the book aside. "I don't like the way you look, lad. What is it about this Miss Roberts that warrants your concern?"

"She came to our offices this morning. She said she had left Boston and come here to seek employment. She requested a few words in our classified section to that effect. She then asked if I could suggest suitable lodging, and I directed her to Mrs. Thoreau's house. I have just been there, and she has not yet appeared, according to Mrs. Thoreau. For the past hour, I have asked at every available place for lodgers, and they have all shaken their heads. I have even been across to the taverns. She was not there, either, and I have saved your hotel as my last resort."

Barnaby's rosy face gleamed and his merry eyes twinkled. "My dear boy, how careless of you!"

"What?" I said, surprised.

He shook his head, his expression teasing. "How could you have been so cruel, sending her to that awful haven of garrulous spinsters, singing their pious hymns, with our splendid, convivial facilities so conveniently at hand?"

"Undoubtedly it was a mistake, Uncle, but I know your prices, and she asked for some inexpensive place. And as she was of a shy and gentle nature, I thought the high spirits and revelry here would be overpowering."

"Indeed," he said. "I would take the contrary view, as the interminable prattling and chattering among the Thoreau women is even more so, to my way of thinking."

"You are probably right, Uncle, and I have already berated myself for falling short of her trust."

His eyebrows lifted. "What trust is that you speak of?"

"Nothing but my own feeling, Uncle. I feel responsible for her welfare. I was the first in Concord to see her."

"Then she must be rather attractive, Oliver, to have jolted you out of your placid ways," he said.

"More than attractive, Uncle Barnaby. The loveliest and most beautiful I have ever seen. Her manner was gentle, her voice soft and melodious, and she was dressed in a splendid fashion I have never before been privileged to see."

Barnaby sighed. "I blame Rufus for this, Oliver. He has kept your nose too close to the grindstone. He has held you blind-folded for too long, and now you are at risk, too vulnerable to the fairer sex."

My cheek twitched. "Little Louisa Alcott told me the same to-day. She noticed I had removed the card Uncle Rufus had placed across from my desk."

Barnaby laughed. " 'Avoid alluring company.' Ah, yes, I've waited years for you to cast it from your sight."

"I cannot claim credit for the courage, Uncle," I said. "Had it not been for my visitor's seeing it, and trying to hide her amuse-ment, I doubt that it ever would have occurred to me."

He pounded his fist into his hand then, grinning, declared, "Now I am convinced at last there is substance to this phantom young lady, who has stirred you up so. I have long hoped, Oliver, that you would pay more attention to the various young ladies in our fair village, and less to getting the news for your uncle."

"Perhaps I have been blind, Uncle. But still, I would give any-thing to know where she is now."

He smote his forehead in mock dismay. "What fools we are! Perhaps she is in our dining room at this moment, Oliver. While you are grieving for her, she is fattening herself up on our cook's excellent veal, lamb, and potatoes."

He took my arm and urged me toward the open dining room. It was not yet full, and it required but one searching glance to see she was not there. "No, Uncle, she is not present."

"A pity, Oliver, but keep up your hope. Perhaps later."

There was one there I did know, and had great distaste for. He sat alone at a rear table, his heavy, florid face wreathed in the smoke of a large cigar in his hand. "Had I known that man was here," I murmured, "despite your superior facilities, I would never have suggested she stay for even a moment."

Barnaby covered his mouth and cleared his throat. "I share your sentiments, Oliver, but I could not refuse him service here on any account. I run a hotel open to the public and cannot be choosy about my customers."

The man smoking the cigar would have recognized me, as we had had differences in the past. But he kept his eyes on his plate, wrapped in his own thoughts, and there was no need for our exchanging greetings.

His name is Gordon Goodfellow, a misnomer as he is hardly that. He is a selectman in our town, but several years ago he was a school board trustee. Henry Thoreau, fresh out of Harvard, had returned to Concord and secured a well-paying position at the public school. But he was averse to flogging his students, and when Goodfellow intruded and insisted that he use the rod, Henry lost his temper. In a rare blind rage, he lined up six innocents at random and beat them severely. One of the unfortunate victims whom he ruthlessly lashed was his mother's house servant, Roxanne. He never returned to the school.

Barnaby saw me to the door. "If she arrives, Oliver, I promise I will hold her here. You might come back tomorrow and find better luck. I'm sorry, lad."

"Tomorrow?" I said. "Where can she have been that long?"

He shrugged, shaking his head. "Women have been known to have a change of heart, Oliver. Perhaps she has had second thoughts and returned to the station. Have you made inquiries there?"

I stared at him. "What? Turn and run so quickly and not give her prospects here sufficient time?"

Barnaby smiled and patted my shoulder. "I'm sorry to have to tell you this, son, but women have a differing notion of logic than men. But now, another thought. The woods are close to the Thoreaus' house. What if she decided to take a walk there? It was a lovely day, and there are many trails."

I nodded, with increasing dismay. "Yes, but they interweave and she might have become lost in them."

"Well then, tomorrow in the light, we can organize a search party. And there is another possibility there. She might have heard of Henry's hut by Walden Pond and thought of seeing him."

"Uncle, I mentioned Henry, and she has not heard of him. Further, if she waits for him, she will wait all night, as he is across the square in jail for refusing to pay his poll tax. Mr. Staples is holding him until tomorrow."

Barnaby smiled. "Ah, well, our Henry must have thorns for his crown. Till tomorrow morning, Oliver, good night." With another reassuring pat on my shoulder, he turned back.

It was with a heavy heart that I returned to the old gray house in Huckleberry Lane where I was raised. My dear aunt Martha had kept my supper warm and did not question my lateness. She knew Uncle Rufus had let me in for extra duties, and was accustomed to us both working long hours at unpredictable times.

But I had no appetite for food and wished somehow the plates could be transported to the Alcott family, where they existed, as I have said, on bread and water, prayer, a random apple or parsnip, and readings from Bronson in Latin.

My good aunt, familiar with my ever-ready appetite, was moved by my apathy to touch my forehead, wondering if I had found a fever. I assured her it was nothing, that I was merely constrained over some disturbing news. She did not pursue the matter and returned to the kitchen, leaving me alone with my dark fears.

I read for a while in my uncle's study, unable to engage my mind with whatever book I selected. It was late when I retired to my room, and much later before my turbulent thoughts admitted sleep.

Wherein a Most Brutal
and Heinous Crime Is Revealed

A harsh and metallic jangling sound woke me from a nightmarish dream in which I was being pursued by various phantom demons. As I struggled to wakefulness, I recognized the source of the disturbance: the village bell inside the courthouse. It is struck only in times of calamity as an urgent warning, and when repeatedly sounded, as now, it bespeaks a special alarm denoting a matter of the gravest importance.

My heart thumped madly as I hurried into my trousers and boots, knowing at once my darkest fears were soon to be realized. I clattered down the steps and threw the door open, stifling a sob that strangled my throat. Barnaby was already there, waiting.

His broad chest was heaving as if he had come at a dead run from his house, and his ruddy face was moist with perspiration. He greeted me without so much as a word, his countenance telling me all, and his hand gripped my arm as if admonishing strength.

"Is it—" I gasped. "Is it her?"

He was turning away, and I stepped after him. "How did you learn of it?" I asked. But he only shook his head, as if loath to answer.

Finally, as we hurried to the main road, he said, "I had sent word to our hunters to search for her. My night clerk had orders to awaken me upon any news from them."

"Then it was in the woods, as you surmised, Barnaby?"

"Aye, at Walden Pond."

It was early dawn, the barren sky gray with only the merest hint of gold behind the hills to the east, and already the old road was alive with men hurrying to the woods. They walked or ran or rode their horses, all of an extreme eagerness to see for themselves what some already knew. Barnaby and I hurried along with them, not a word more between us. Doors and windows opened as we passed, and gray-faced men and women stared silently at us. Some children tried to slip out the doors and join us but were firmly held, then pulled back inside, the doors closing at once.

Shortly we came to the end of the village. Here at the fork in the road, we were joined by men hurrying down the Lincoln Road, which runs close by Walden Pond, as alert to the village bell as our own townspeople. The near meadows were being trampled into wide, irregular paths, and Barnaby and I began to trot now as we heard shouts from those already in the woods.

Thoreau had built his small hut on the south side of a slope over a deep cove, protected from the winds, deep in a blackberry pasture with a fine view of the pond a few hundred feet away. There was a line of men strung from the hut to the pond, staring down, reluctant to move any farther. With great impatience, Barnaby and I surged against their unyielding bodies. Finally we had to forcibly make our way through, roughly knocking aside the most stubborn who defied us entry. Our townspeople can be quite mulish and ugly when provoked, and venomous words were directed at our backs as at last we broke through. For this, I cared nothing, as I was in a rough, unreasoning mood myself.

Sheriff Staples was already there, and, surprisingly, so was Thoreau. He was kneeling on one leg, hunched over the sprawled, inert body lying at his doorstep, looking as intently down at her as if he were the coroner.

I saw the parasol on the ground close to the still form and could not take another step forward. A line of rough, strong men stood nearby, rigid and ashen, staring down dumbly at the violated form. Barnaby was moving away from me, his upper body hunched forward with great intensity, but I stayed still, as if paralyzed.

The strange runic chant I had heard from Hetta sounded once more inside my head.

One from near,
one from far,
mischief done

by morning star,
The wooded lair
to doom is wed,
and damp the hair
of gold turned red.

Barnaby was hunkered over the ruined figure, his shoulder next to Thoreau's, shaking his head. He then looked up and, not seeing me at his side, turned in my direction. He saw me, rooted and transfixed, mouthed some words, and waved his arm, beckoning. Seeing me then unwilling or unable to step forward, he sprung to his feet. He hurried toward me, his face of a high color, shaking his leonine head as if perplexed.

He was shouting, but blood pounding in my brain made me deaf. The details matter not, I thought, turning away, my body slack and ready to fall, riddled with a consternation I had truly never before experienced.

Barnaby's strong hand clasped my arm roughly and shook me. His red face was so close to mine, the purple veins on his nose were visible, his breath strong and warm.

"Oliver," he was shouting hoarsely, "it is not who you thought. It is our poor demented soul Hetta."

I stared dumbly at him, my eyes filming unwillingly. "What are you saying?" I said feebly.

Again he shook me, bringing life to my bones. "It is Hetta," he repeated. "Hetta Bird, who has been so savagely murdered. Oliver, will you listen—it is not your Miss Roberts."

"What?" I said again, reluctant to confront death's reality. "But—how?"

He was prodding me forward, impatient with my limpness. "Bashed over the head, it seems. An ugly wound. Come see for yourself."

In Which the Mystery
of the Vile Murder and
the Missing Girl Is Protracted

Moments later, I stared purblind from bent knee at the hapless woman. There was a great bloody gash across her brow. Her cloudy gray eyes gazed unseeing into space. Her gray hair, which the blood from her brutal wound had turned crimson, streamed loosely under her head.

A strange growling note issued from my throat. While only a seeming instant before I had been filled with unutterable, voiceless sorrow, now I was engorged with a fierce rage.

Pounding the ground with my fist, I ranted in a voice I had never before used. "Who could have done this vile thing?" I cried. "Who is so unfeeling as to have harmed this poor, unstable soul so dear to our hearts!"

Through the film of my tears, I saw scuffling feet and looked up. There stood the thin line of hunters who had found her—hard, stolid men, disturbed now by my inclement emotion. Men I know well: the one-eyed fisherman, George Melvin. The muskrat trapper, John Goodwin. Humphrey Buttrick, the bear hunter. The young Indian tracker, Charley Bigbow. Looking into their hard, unwavering eyes, it was impossible to tell who had found Hetta. I knew that it mattered not, and felt ashamed that in some perverse way I should be grateful.

Barnaby, at my side, stepped closer. Then, leaning over, he did what I should have done and could not, gently closing her unseeing eyes.

"God rest you, Hetta," he said tonelessly. "Now and forever, you will be at peace."

The rough men beyond muttered a ragged "Amen."

Barnaby addressed Sheriff Staples then, his voice uneven with anger. "Well, Sam, it would appear we have a murderer here in Concord. What do you propose to do about this foul and shameful deed?"

Sheriff Staples's yellow eyes flickered with a strange inner light, seemed to glow for a moment, then became dull again. He found his pipe and knocked some dottle from it on his thick hand. "I've looked at the body, Mr. Fields," he said slowly. "The rigor has left, and my guess is she's been dead past twelve hours, sir. As for the murderer among us, as you suggest, the only one I can say for certain didn't do this awful deed would be our own Mr. Thoreau here. He has been with us since early yesterday morning until a while ago when I heard the news. I released him then over his objections and we came down here to the pond together. As for who might have done it, I cannot say other than time will tell more, and lead us to the guilty party."

Barnaby cleared his throat and spoke drily. "Yes, Sam, you

have made a good start. It is indeed a relief to know our Henry is not a suspect. You are a good policeman, Mr. Staples, but I fear you may have to extend yourself more in this instance. Time alone solves nothing. It is no fault of your own, but perhaps this issue of a vicious murder is beyond your usual capabilities to deal with. If you agree, perhaps it would do no harm for us to call in the Boston police, who assuredly must have investigators suitably trained for an evil matter such as this."

Staples frowned and dug at the ground with the toe of his boot. "Please have patience, Mr. Fields. As you say, I have no expertise in matters like this, and no doubt Boston has the men as can do better. But let us wait until Dr. Ripple comes to examine the body. After he has given me his best judgment, I will know better how to proceed." His hand gestured to the still body. "Right fond of Hetta I was in me own way, never harmed a soul to my knowing. You can rest assured that I'll do what needs the doing."

Barnaby shook his head in exasperation. "Yes, but there is more to be done than what is evident here, Sam. A young woman is missing. A visitor from Boston who arrived here but yesterday. Her name is Margaret Roberts."

Sam Staples shook his head, squinting fiercely. "This is news to me, Mr. Fields. I'll need to know more."

Barnaby wagged his thumb back to me. "I think you had better talk to Oliver. He is the sole witness to her arrival and can tell you more."

As I got to my feet, Thoreau glanced at me and said, "The man's a fool. Tell him nothing."

"I'm sorry, Henry," I said. "I fear I must. The hunters were looking for her and found Hetta instead."

Thoreau did not respond, and I thought the matter done with. But I saw his attention was elsewhere. He was holding a small twig in a gloved hand and, I noticed now, was flicking bits of dirt and grass from Hetta's shawl and blouse.

The anger and despair I felt left no room for my customary formal address. "Henry, what on earth are you doing?" I said.

He did not reply but rather looked closer at the slender leaf on the twig. He nodded to himself, studying it carefully.

"As you know, Oliver, I have always maintained that the leaf is the overall manifestation of life. In this instance, it is the opposite. It has a name, *Conium maculatum*. It is commonly called winter fern, spotted parsley, spotted cowbane, and poison hemlock."

I stared impatiently at him. "Hemlock? Really, Henry, I have no time for a dissertation on plants—"

"But this is how she was murdered," Thoreau said.

Barnaby raised his voice. "Oliver, will you come here, please, and explain to Mr. Staples?"

I raised my hand. "In a moment, Uncle."

"In this instance," Thoreau said, "poison hemlock. You are familiar, of course, with the best known of its victims, Socrates of Athens—"

"Mr. Thoreau," I said, "perhaps you cannot see the trees for the flowers. It is quite obvious to me that the blow here on Hetta's head caused her demise. What conceivable reason have you to introduce some other source for her murder?"

His arm swept upward. "The thickets up there are alive with it." He brushed small white flowers from Hetta's throat and small gray-green seeds that had collected on her shawl. He held these to my face, and I drew back, repulsed. "Yes, they have a dis-agreeable, mousy odor," he said.

Barnaby's voice sounded again. "Oliver!"

"Excuse me, Mr. Thoreau," I said. I picked up the parasol and lifted it under his nose. "Since you are indeed such a blood-hound, smell this then. This parasol I saw last in the hand of a young woman from Boston, visiting here. It belonged to her, not to Hetta. And Margaret Roberts has been missing since I saw her last, yesterday morning. When you can explain to me how the parasol came to be in Hetta Bird's possession, then will I listen to your discourse on the properties of poison hemlock."

Before he could respond to my angry words, I walked away to join Barnaby and Sam Staples. There I again related the story of Margaret Roberts, to the full extent that I knew it. Staples lis-tened without interruption, and when I had finished, I showed him the parasol.

"This belonged to Miss Roberts, Sam. There must be some reason why it has been found here, and how it came into the possession of poor Hetta. And while I am not inclined to inter-fere with your search for Hetta's murderer, I am equally urgently asking you to continue a search for Miss Roberts. Perhaps she is lost somewhere in these woods, or worse, foul play has befallen her, too. Indeed, Sheriff, I am of the same opinion as my uncle, that perhaps it would be wise for you to engage the services of the Boston police."

Staples nodded gravely. "Rest assured, Oliver, I will see to it that justice is done. We will scour these woods for your missing young lady, since that is a higher priority now. It will be no worse for Hetta Bird, certainly. And one will lead to the other, more likely than not."

He walked then with purposeful steps toward the group of trackers and hunters.

Barnaby was patting my shoulder. "Do not despair, Oliver. Those men know their game. They will scour every thicket to find her, never fear."

"The only possibility I can think of, Uncle Barnaby, is that she changed her mind somehow and took the next train back to Boston."

He looked at his watch, a handsome embossed gold time-piece. "I must return to the hotel, lad," he said. "I'll make an inquiry at the station and, when next I see you, will report on that possibility."

With that, he clasped my hand warmly again, patted my head as he had done so many times in my childhood, and turned back to the village center.

Thoreau was still scraping flowers and leaves off Hetta's worn, frayed garments. I squatted next to him, wondering if it was worthwhile to pursue his singular theory.

"I'm sorry to have been rude, Henry," I said softly, aiming to placate him. "I will be happy to listen to your theory now, odd as it may seem."

His luminous eyes regarded mine, and his countenance was

most grave as he nodded. "I am not disputing the possibility that this blow to her head was fatal. Dr. Ripple will perhaps establish that as a fact when he arrives, and I respect his judgment in these matters. But why then these marks on her throat, evidence of attempted strangulation—and these dried seeds and flowers of the poison hemlock?" He held a handful of the musty, odorous plant for me to see.

I shook my head. "Henry, I am confused, sir."

He waved his arm to the forest. "The woods are full of these plants near Hetta's hut. But she knew as much as I, or more, of the properties of all plants. Hetta, of all people, would not have been eating these seeds. She would not have been a willing victim to their inexorable, slow death, as was Socrates. No, some person tried to force them down her throat, and perhaps succeeded."

"Yes, you may be right then. The poor woman was deranged but never suicidal."

Thoreau nodded. "I find it strange, too, Oliver, that she lies here, stilled by death, placed on my doorstep, when it is obvious she was murdered elsewhere and then carried here to rest on Walden Pond."

"Is that another conjecture, Henry, or can you establish that as fact?" I inquired.

Thoreau shrugged his thin shoulders. "Look at the ground here. You will find no marks of a struggle. For a person to be strangled out of her life, we would expect a multitude of footprints, from both the victim and her attacker. As you can plainly see, this earth is hardly disturbed, as if nothing untoward has taken place here. There is even scant evidence of the blood lost from the gash to her head."

I stared dumbly at him, startled beyond words. The hunters had said nothing of this.

"Do you see other marks of the young woman who has disappeared, Henry? She came here yesterday from Boston, was with me briefly in my office, and then disappeared on her way to lodge at your mother's house, as I had suggested."

He shook his head. "I have seen nothing yet, Oliver, but I promise I will look around carefully."

Conversation with Charley Bigbow, a Neglected Friend—to the Shame of the Narrator

Sheriff Staples provided the hunters with the description I gave him of Margaret Roberts and urged them to search the woods again. Awaiting the arrival of Dr. Ripple, he busied himself searching the ground for clues, studying footprints.

I was wavering, torn between searching the woods myself and my commitment to my uncle Rufus to return to the office with the news of the murder. Staring into space for guidance, I noticed one tracker remained. He was leaning slackly against the side of Thoreau's hut, his dark eyes fixed upon me. With shame and warmth commingled, I recognized the stalwart figure of the aforementioned Charley Bigbow, the Indian youth I have known since childhood yet had not seen or spoken to for years.

There are about a dozen Algonquin Indian families in Concord, about the same number of blacks, and they all live off the main road near the river in the same tawdry shanties as the

Irish. Charley had been an exceptionally keen student but, more often than not, was forced to miss class to help his father in the fields. Bronson Alcott always found time to tutor any of these racially tormented children at his school, and his home as well. Whatever Charley missed in our class, it was to his advantage, as with Bronson he learned Latin as well.

He was forced to quit school completely before his final year in order to help support his family. He worked at so many different jobs I finally lost track of him, and only recently he had become a local figure of some prominence, due to his uncanny skills at finding children who were lost in the woods. There is no need for bloodhounds with Charley Bigbow around. I have no idea how well rewarded he is for saving the lives of the lost tots, but far more important for him is the grateful regard so many hold for him now, and he is no longer just another pariah Indian for our ignorant townspeople to hold in contempt.

"Charley," I said, gripping his hand, then walked several paces away from Staples with him. His brown eyes gleamed with a watchful amusement, and he waited patiently until I spoke.

"Charley," I said, "am I to assume that you discovered Hetta's body here at the same time as John, George, and Humphrey?"

He nodded and said, "Yes, boss."

"Is that not an odd coincidence, that you all found her simultaneously?"

"No, boss," he said softly. "It just happen."

"Did you all enter the forest at the same place, then?"

He shook his head. "No, boss. Nobody know where she is, so we take different way."

"And yet you expect me to believe that you all came out at the same time and found her here, all breaking through the woods at once?"

He nodded, amused. "Yes, boss. You no think possible?"

I shook my head, eyeing him suspiciously. "Yes, I no think possible. And for God's sake, Charley, why do you persist in this witless noble savage manner of speech, when we both know you can speak as well as I?"

He broke into a sudden, wide smile, exposing a perfect row of gleaming teeth. "Oh, that," he said casually. "I thought you knew that around here they don't like us Indians to speak your language properly. More to the point, they are not inclined to give us work unless we remember our proper place, which is, as you must know, to be submissive, not speak our minds, and say 'Yes, boss.' So you might say it's a habit I've grown into, to save my hide and ensure my not being lynched."

"Proper place!" I said indignantly. "You're one of the few genuine Americans in the village."

"Right, Oliver," he said soothingly. "But inasmuch as everybody else is ignorant of that fact, I prefer to keep it secret. I don't mind really. There aren't very many people available to have a proper conversation and meeting of the minds with anyhow."

I shook my head. "Oh, Charley, I am so sorry. I've let myself lose track of you down through the years, and somehow assumed that you were doing well."

"It's all relative, Oliver," he said. "I live a healthy outdoor life, and don't make enough money to get drunk on. I've seen you looking better, so tell me how I can help you, as I can plainly see you're distraught over the missing girl."

"It is double mischief, Charley. Hetta's murder and the disappearance of Margaret Roberts, whom I met but briefly. To tell the truth, I am in shock because I was prepared to believe the body I would find here would be that of the girl, not poor Hetta."

He studied my face carefully. "Perhaps you will explain, Oliver. I've never known you to fantasize."

"Indeed, it was Hetta herself who thus prepared me," I said, and then, seeing him frown with disbelief, I told him of our meeting on the old Lexington Road and Hetta's insistence on a prophecy meant to involve me, followed immediately by her runic incantation. I recited it word for word.

Charley nodded. "I noticed your arrival here. You apparently saw the parasol first near the body and assumed the worst. I could see you change color and tremble at this distance. Hetta prepared you well, Oliver. I also would have succumbed to the fright and gloom of those remarkable words she set in rhyme for you."

"She had never before made a prophecy for me, but I have heard of others, as you must have yourself, Charley. Confused as poor Hetta was, she has always managed to frighten me, since early childhood."

"She had me intimidated, too," Charley said. "But then I thought only Indians were superstitious and believed in prophecy. Our tribes have always been in thrall to our elders and medicine men."

"Well, then," I said, "I'm relieved to know you could be as

susceptible, Charley. Now, let me tell you all that I know of Margaret Roberts, and then perhaps we can logically interpret the meaning behind her disappearance, the fact that her parasol was found with Hetta's body, and the manner and reason for Hetta's murder."

He heard me out as I reviewed the complete circumstances of my office transaction with Miss Roberts, including, as well, the brief discussion with the observant Louisa May.

Charley smiled. "Undoubtedly Louisa May has a gifted imagination, but to have left such an impression, your Miss Roberts must be quite beautiful."

"Yes. Extremely."

"Intelligent, too, since you removed the sign Uncle Rufus placed there to lessen her ridicule."

"It's been there for years, Charley. Honestly, I'd forgotten all about it. And Miss Roberts seemed to believe me when I told her as much. Now you have it all, and I will listen to your accounting of Hetta's murder first, and then of your search through the woods without finding trace of the girl."

He shrugged his thick shoulders. "These are not virgin woods, Oliver. Remember, we played here ourselves. To follow three separate fresh tracks in the bad light was difficult."

"Three?" I said. "How three?"

"Your missing girl, Hetta, and the assailant. Most likely, Miss Roberts became lost in the woods, then—alarmed at being followed—panicked in the undergrowth and lost her parasol to some thicket too dense for her to hide in.

"She must have run on without it. Hetta lives in and roams

this forest. She found the parasol. You know Hetta, how she would put on airs given the chance. Now if our murderer loses sight of Miss Roberts, and sees another figure with the parasol, he assumes it is his original quarry and attacks her. Perhaps not with the blow to the head. That may have been dealt later."

"Thoreau has also suggested that theory."

"Well, Henry would. The hemlock leaves and berries, flowers, and poisonous seeds are there if one knows what to see. The amount she was made to swallow is immaterial. It doesn't take much hemlock for a fatal dose. Hetta would struggle, he would try to strangle her, and then to settle the matter he would find a stone and beat her down with it."

"Thoreau also theorized that, after she was killed, Hetta was carried here. Why would the murderer do that?"

"Perhaps his intention was to leave her body in Walden Pond, where it would be found much later. Or he might have changed his mind, leaving her at Henry's door to incriminate him. When we find him, perhaps he will explain his devious motive."

"What motive had he then to follow Miss Roberts?"

Charley smiled. "Perhaps she can shed some light on that matter, as well, when we find her." He shook his head. "Frankly, Oliver, your mystery starts with her. I find it hard to believe her story of coming here solely to change her luck, to take any employment offered without use of her own experience. If your eyes were not turned to mush, you would see that."

"Admittedly it has troubled me, Charley, despite her beauty and charm. If it is possible to become so unbalanced as to fall in love instantly, then I plead guilty. If we ever find her, you will understand."

"She could be anywhere, Oliver. Hiding still in the woods, or perhaps already gone through them. She could be on her way to Sudbury or even back to Boston."

Struck by a dismaying thought, I cried, "Unless this monster, whoever he is, has already dealt with her after discovering his mistake with Hetta!"

Charley then addressed me sternly, his nostrils flaring. "Fie on your morbid thinking, Oliver! How can you profess to be so unalterably in love and at the same moment envision death? It is unseemly of you, and contrary to your optimistic nature."

I bowed my head, my voice broken. "Because I am afraid, Charley, and unable to throttle my anxiety. If I only had some tangible indication of her movement, her ability to escape this madman's sinister stalking, I might be able then to envision her survival."

His brown hand dipped into his pocket, and he withdrew it, opening his palm. "Well, I found this not far from Hetta's hut. Would it have meaning for you?"

It was a small pearl button softly glowing in his large hand. "Why, that is from her frock, I am sure of it," I said with excitement.

"Torn loose by her struggle through the thickets," Charley said. "And then there is this, which I found deeper into the woods."

He thrust the object out from beneath his coat. It was the

same tawny Tuscan hat the girl had been wearing. He placed it upon his head, grinning like a fool, forcing me to laugh at its incongruity.

"That's her hat, Charley! I have seen no other in this village like it."

He handed it to me. "I was afraid you would say that, Oliver. I was thinking of wearing it to church. I'm sure it looks good on me."

I folded it carefully into my pocket. "You are quite wrong about that. But how did you come by this?"

"It was snagged on a blackberry bush farther along. The proof, Oliver, that your lady was moving fast, intent upon escape. So do not despair."

I gripped his hand. "I thank you, dear friend. I cannot in good conscience urge you to continue your search while I must return to my work. But Uncle Rufus has gone to New York and is depending on me to run his newspaper." He nodded and was turning away when I stopped him. "Charley, we must talk again. Aunt Martha misses you, and it would please her greatly if you could come to dinner tonight. You can have the plate of Uncle Rufus."

Charley smiled and thumped my shoulder. "I miss your aunt myself, Oliver. If you can persuade her not to go overboard, it would please me greatly to dine with you again. Perhaps by then I will have better news for you."

I shook my head. "One is not contingent upon the other. Please come, regardless of the search."

Charley nodded. "I'll really miss that hat," he said. "Are you sure it's hers?"

"It's only the feather in it that you like," I said. "The Indian in you."

"Well, that, too," he said. He waved his hand and in a moment had disappeared in the woods.

A Visit to the Higher Realms of Thought with Ralph Waldo Emerson, to the Profit of the Narrator, Despite His Inequity in the Exchange

For the remainder of the morning, I lost myself in a protracted effort to write down and editorialize on the wanton murder of Hetta Bird, allowing my deep emotions full play in attempting to call attention to an unforgivable crime, this senseless assault on a harmless creature. In my fury, my words and thoughts overreached until I realized at length that I had now exalted Hetta to the status of local saint. I had to lay down my pencil ruefully then and reconsider, knowing how Uncle Rufus would regard this emotional reaction. It was a reflection of my own childish affronts to Hetta and subsequent guilt that caused me to romanticize her so. Now I had to look at the matter more objectively.

I revised and rewrote until my fury had cooled sufficiently to encompass the deed itself without further elaboration. The effort was doubly complicated by my refusal to allow thoughts of Margaret Roberts and her disappearance to surface. To do so would have reduced my throbbing brain to utter helplessness, and I bit my lip to help me achieve more objectivity.

In this mood of trying to remove myself from my feelings, I frowned with impatience at a sound from the door. When I saw it was Mr. Emerson inviting himself into my office, my jaw sagged, and all pretense at control left me, since to my mind this was the nearest equivalent of a visitation from God. I could only stare in helpless astonishment, as at a fleeting miracle bestowed on my behalf at a time when comfort was most needed.

"Ah, Oliver," he said, "I do hope you will pardon this intrusion. I simply must see you, and there is no other way around it."

In all of New England, and most certainly in Concord, our most godly representative is Mr. Ralph Waldo Emerson, and no man alive at this time would quarrel with that. He is at all times the most generous and forbearing of any citizen. Humble and yet majestic, he is a seer who inspires all who have heard his words or read his essays to strive for the betterment of their lives and souls. This is in accord with his doctrine of Self-Reliance and his sublime thoughts concerning the Over-Soul, which makes all men one. He is only fourteen years older than Thoreau, but the distance between them is as the distance from here to a star in the heavens. When in his presence, one becomes a reverent disciple, eager to please and absorb his masterful wisdom and celestial vision.

Emerson, one of the few who dared confront public opinion,

recently had decided to speak out against slavery, despite attempts to stifle his freedom of speech. Almost every hall in Boston was closed to those of Abolitionist sentiment, and every church but one. In Concord it was the same, and the Lyceum would not admit his lecture. Finally the Trinitarian Congregational Church permitted him to use its vestry, and to the discomfort of many, he insisted upon New England's sacred duty to allow the free discussion of any matter pertaining to the rights of man.

In 1838, our nation's duplicity had aroused him when President Van Buren ordered the removal of the entire nation of Cherokees from its homeland in Georgia. As the eighteen thousand Indians were dragged over mountains and across rivers beyond the Mississippi to a wilderness unlike the fields and villages they had left behind, thousands to perish on the journey, Emerson's was our only voice raised in outrage. He wrote in our paper and sent an indignant letter to the president, calling attention to this crime against human nature. His message on morality proclaimed loudly on national errors and broken faith.

So I wondered now if his visit was in aid of one or another of these causes.

Finding my voice, I said, "Good morning, sir."

"Well, good morning, Oliver," he replied in his firm and pleasant tones, hesitating between words in his usual manner as he plucked the correct ones from his vocabulary. "I wonder if I might ask a favor of you."

Knowing full well he disliked fawning as a craven act, and yet trying to conceal my own tendency to do so, I found sufficient voice to respond simply. "With pleasure, Mr. Emerson. How may I help you?"

"I would like to use the offices of your uncle's newspaper to insert a personal advertisement. Would this be possible in whatever space you might have available for other than your more noteworthy news?"

"There should be no problem in that regard, sir," I said, "as most of our noteworthy news at the moment, as you phrase it, is indeed to the contrary. Perhaps, in fact, your advertisement will give our pages more flavor, and be an added inducement to awaken our more comatose citizens."

His intensely blue eyes sparkled, and then, since he never permitted himself to laugh out loud and always repressed the impulse instead, the following phenomenon occurred: with his mouth closed, the explosion found its way between his nostrils and eyebrows in a half-suppressed convulsion that betrayed all his features.

In a trice, the groundswell was completed and he found his voice again. "Well," he said, looking down carefully at me, still frozen in my chair. "Oh, well spoken, Oliver. I have quite forgotten your incorruptible tendency to have your own focused insight on our, as you rightfully suggest, laggard community. I must remember to pass your observation along to Bronson, who believes he has already done the Lord's work, at times." He hesitated. "With your permission, of course, Oliver."

I could not suppress a wide grin. "My pleasure, sir."

"To your uncle as well, to ensure his continuing satisfaction with your alertness. Is he around?"

"He is away on business, Mr. Emerson. To Boston, and New York City. I am carrying on for him the next few days. When he returns, I hope he will share your assessment of my alacrity."

He rubbed his prominent, bony nose, nodding. "Of that, I have no doubt. Now as to the matter that has brought me here. I will give you the gist of it, and you may then paraphrase or word it properly to ensure my intention."

I found my pencil and poised it above an order sheet. "I'll write it as you speak, and then perhaps we can formulate it to your specific needs while you are here."

"Whatever you suggest, Oliver. God has given me the seeing eye but not the working hand. Finding the proper words to express my meaning is always most arduous even as I write in my own journal. But let us proceed.

"As you may already know, my eyesight is always a problem. At one time, I had nearly lost it, but an operation proved to be all that was needed for restoration. Now it is waning again. Since my work entails a great deal of writing and reading, I find myself in much difficulty with one or the other, with no mind to neglect either. It has occurred to me that, if I were to find somebody to read for me—*to* me, more likely—my sight would then be spared for the writing end of it.

"Therefore, what I wish described in your advertisement is this distinct need. I am looking for a respectable young lady with a pleasant voice and demeanor who might be willing to accept such employment."

The pencil dropped from my hand and rolled on the paper as I recoiled in dismay at his words.

"Why, Oliver," he exclaimed, with much concern, "what is the matter? Are you ill, my boy?"

It required a long and unendurable moment for me to recover from the most wretched feeling that an icy dagger had been plunged into me. My thoughts heretofore had always been of the mind rather than of the heart, but now I was enveloped by a cold and desolate condition I knew not how to parry. The ghost of Margaret Roberts had claimed my attention and settled over me with an insistent presence, stifling my breath.

At last the ominous sensation passed, and I was able to speak. "No, sir, not ill, but reacting to the words you have expressed. Yesterday morning, a young lady visited this office. She had come from Boston to seek employment here. She asked me to insert a few words in our classified pages saying simply this: 'Respectable young lady seeks situation.' In addition to the pleasant voice and demeanor you require, she had exceptional beauty, as well as great intelligence."

Mr. Emerson looked at me with a puzzled expression. "I am slow-witted this morning, Oliver, and beg your understanding. She would seem to meet my conditions, and yet you temporize with me."

"Not willfully, sir," I said, "but I find the words difficult. The young lady I described is missing, and reported to be in the vicinity of a heinous crime. Miss Hetta Bird, poor soul, was found murdered this morning at Walden Pond, near Henry's hut. Almost the entire village was there to satisfy its morbid curiosity."

Emerson clapped a hand to his long brown hair in dismay. "I

was asleep and thought I heard some commotion, as if from a great distance, but I remained in my bed and have spoken to nobody since arising. Murdered, you said? Here in our tranquil town?"

"It will not be so tranquil again for a long while," I said. "Those of the many who were there will keep it afresh in their minds, an obscene atrocity not to be forgotten." I stirred the papers on my desk. "I was writing my editorial on the matter as you were on your way here. As for the missing girl, I fear her dead, too, but have been too overcome to accept its possibility yet and write of her fate." My voice quivered. "Her grace and loveliness were such that, in the brief moment she was here, I lost my heart to her completely. I feel the utmost dread for her life."

His hand hovered over my shoulder but did not touch it. "I am so terribly sorry, Oliver. Here I have broken my cardinal rule, never to leave my study until four in the afternoon, and have managed to stir your memory afresh in its grief for it. Perhaps I should return another day when you are more composed. There is no imperative on this matter, it is of no grave necessity."

"You could not have known," I said, "and I am sorry to have burdened you with my own affairs." I reclaimed my pencil and the order sheet. "I will be able to sort this out according to your wishes, Mr. Emerson. You need not bother to wait. But if you like, after it is composed properly, I can bring it to your house, and make any correction or adjustment you wish."

He waved his pale hand. "There is no need, Oliver, as I trust your judgment." He hesitated and rubbed his nose, about to leave yet undecided. "I have some experience with the loss of a loved one, Oliver, and perhaps can offer some words that may help lessen your suffering. But only if you are agreeable."

"How could I not be in response to your compassionate offer?" I said. "I remember a few years back, when your little boy Waldo died in his fifth year. I cared to offer my condolences to you then but refrained for fear of intruding into your personal grief. So I do not merit the thoughts you mean to help me with, but nevertheless do indeed welcome what you intend to say with all my heart."

"Well, then," he said with a vigorous nodding of his head, "let us begin. I am no stranger to death in my own family: my father, a sister, and my brothers, save William and poor Bulkeley. The deepest loss was my wife, Ellen, less than a year and a half after we were married. I suffered with that deprival for years, and in fact it turned me from God. She was too good, too sweet, too gentle and warmly intelligent to be taken so from me, I lamented.

"In time, my tears dried and I recovered to my new life here with Lidian. And here was little Waldo, the most dear and precious child in all the world, so it seemed to us, taken from our hearts at such a tender age.

"As you might imagine, we were stricken as if paralyzed. How could this be in the world of bounteous Nature I have sought to glorify with every word I speak or write? But then I thought of it, and it may shock you to hear it, but I said, Well, now it is done and it does not matter. I said it to his mother, Lidian, and she stared at me, as you do now."

"I do apologize, Mr. Emerson," I said. "Truly the words are difficult to accept, with all due respect."

"Yes," he said, his visage grim and unyielding, "but if I had not spoken them, and yet thought it so, we would have remained shattered, prisoners to a love that was too possessive and unreasonable to logic and the natural order of things.

"You see," he continued, "it was only by pressing through this reluctance to accept reality, and choosing to go forward rather than wither ourselves in grief, that we obtained the result. It was a kind of tranquillity, an absolute and undeniable assurance of a higher, more sublime direction. And so I say to you, you must also listen and obey the law of the unconscious. You must surrender your personal self to the spontaneous life within you. Let your nature flow with the river of the universe. There is a common light which touches and enlightens all. You may correctly think of it as divine reason, the unity that lies forever at the base of things, always obedient to the divine laws of the One, the Over-Soul. Look within yourself, Oliver."

I sat stunned, with glazed eyes, mesmerized by his melodious voice and sweeping phrases, which I could not trust my ears to follow. It was my first experience of a personal lecture from Emerson, and there was nothing for me to say in response, as his elevated thoughts had humbled me to speechlessness.

Then he was leaning over me, his great nose scant inches from mine, his eyes direct and unwavering. "What is the charge for the advertisement you will place for me?"

I blinked, looked down at the order sheet, and counted the

words. "It will come to three lines, for which the charge is fifty cents."

He reached into his pocket, withdrew some coins, and tossed them on my desk. "There you are, Oliver. I do appreciate the time you have allowed me to spend with you."

Before I could answer, his black coat rustled and he was through the door. He drew it closed behind him, not softly, as some do, but with a vigorous thrust, as if I had awakened something within him that needed a vehement assertion, lest Emerson himself should forget and turn to putty as mortal, weaker men can do.

Concerning a Visit to Dr. Amos Cornelius Ripple in Order to Confirm the Manner of Hetta Bird's Death by a Person Unknown

The many long pages I drafted and revised, only to discard and attempt again, proved to be my salvation in occupying my mind while I waited for word about Margaret Roberts. It had seemed such a surety that Charley and the other hunters would have found her by the late hours of the afternoon, and yet I heard nothing.

At long last I finally had managed a sober account of the tragedy at Walden Pond, in the detached and objective manner rigorously enforced by my uncle Rufus. I threw down my pencil, collected the pages and locked them up in type for the printer, and left the office.

It was time to settle the matter of how Hetta had been murdered. While Thoreau's theory of the poisoning by hemlock had been given credence by Charley Bigbow, it seemed too bizarre for me to accept. The blow on her head would have been as conclusive and far easier to manage. I simply could not conceive of the notion that she had been forced to swallow the deadly berries, no more than I could imagine the mind of a murderer with such an unorthodox design for his victim. By this time, our Dr. Ripple would most certainly have made his diagnosis, and whatever opinion he held would be sound and acceptable to me without qualification.

It was a short walk beyond the church to the old Colonial house where he lived, on a rutted road at the crest of a hill. It was the good doctor himself who brought me into the world and saw me through the coughs and fevers of my childhood.

As I drew closer to the narrow old house, my heart proclaimed new anxieties by its increased beat. The thought had just occurred to me that, perhaps without my knowledge, he had received word of another victim found in the woods. A young woman of pleasing looks wearing a brown frock missing a small pearl button.

His ancient buggy stood outside the slatted gate, and the familiar sorrel mare called Doris rested contentedly in harness, munching on fallen apples. She was easily fifteen years old, but her pace had not slowed noticeably as she carried Dr. Ripple on his rounds, no matter the weather or time of day or night. Perhaps the mare always knew she would be long in service and had been deliberate and studied in her gait from the start to ensure her dependability in later years.

"Doris," I exclaimed with much affection, stroking her nose, "you look as beautiful as ever." She lifted her head to regard me more closely, and I picked a sound apple off the ground and offered it to her, and she devoured it without a whinny of gratitude. Then, ignoring me, she found one of her own choosing, apparently not impressed by my kindness, and chomped on it with her great teeth. "Mine was a better one," I said in passing, to no effect. It has always been said of this gentle animal that she has no favorites and calmly accepts our caresses as her due.

The doctor's housekeeper must have noted my approach, as the door opened before I had touched it. Miss Emily Avery, middle-aged but still red-cheeked and robust, stared at me and fell back a step. "Why, it's young Oliver Puckle, is it not? My dear, how you have grown."

"It is more than ten years since I was here last, Miss Emily," I said. "These things happen. And you yourself seem younger somehow."

"Well, I do keep," she said laughing, "but hardly as you describe it." Her hand reached out to touch my cheek. "You are so fair, Oliver, and remindful of your mother."

"You knew her? I have forgotten she had friends here and, due to the circumstances of my birth, never dared to think about her earlier life."

Miss Avery frowned. "Then it's the doing of your uncle Rufus and his singular, unforgiving nature that has denied you the proper right of any child to curiosity. If your aunt Martha did not fear his black temper, she would have told you many things. She dared not, I'm sure, to spare Rufus the reminder of his sister's folly."

"Was it indeed folly, then, do you think?"

She shook her head, her lips pressed firmly together. "No, it was not folly, Oliver. It was love for an attractive scoundrel."

"You knew him, too?" I said, surprised.

She smiled, closing her eyes, leaning limply back against the open door. "Ah, did I not! Desmond Defoe, what a picture of a man! They say it was his drinking drove them apart, but it was more than that. It was his love of life and freedom." Again her head shook. "A wild horse must run, Oliver, and that's the truth of it."

I stared. "I am grateful for what you have told me, Miss Emily," I said, "and perhaps I can talk more with you concerning my parents another time. But now I must speak to Dr. Ripple, if he is in."

A pale hand waved from an open door in the gloomy interior, and then I heard the doctor's voice. "Indeed he is, Oliver. I thought Emily would keep you out there all the day. Do come in, son."

He led me into his consulting room, shook my hand, and offered me a chair, which I declined. The doctor is perhaps in his late seventies, spare and erect, his long face seamed with lines, but still with a full head of hair, white and long, flowing to his shoulders. His deep-set eyes are gray and steady, and his voice has become cracked with time, as it needs more air from his thin chest.

"Trouble with your tonsils again, Oliver?" he asked. He stepped behind his desk, pulled an old notebook out from under a pile, and began stirring the pages. "I remember treating you for that last time, and expected another similar flare-up."

"That was more than ten years ago, Dr. Ripple," I said, smiling. "My tonsils have been fine since you cauterized them. It is not ill health that brings me here, sir."

"Well, I am relieved to hear that," he said, closing his thick, musty book. "But," he added, rising from his chair, "since you are here now, perhaps you will allow me to examine your throat again and settle the matter. Then we can discuss whatever else has brought you here, my boy."

He came toward me then with a slender wooden probe before I could voice objection. Childlike, I did not resist his urging tap on my lips and opened my mouth obediently.

Placing the probe lightly on my tongue, he peered inside with no further ado. "It is always a comfort to me to see how nature will in time heal my blundering efforts, and this instance is no exception. Those tonsils, and your teeth, will probably outlive you, Oliver, and you need have no further problems." He tossed the probe into a basket on the floor. "Ten years, you say? A remarkable recovery, as I thought surely we would lose you then to the infection and fever."

"If I did not thank you then, Dr. Ripple, I do now, sir. It was long ago, I've forgotten the incident."

"Fine," he said briskly, rubbing his hands together. "Although if I recall correctly, it is your aunt Martha who deserves the credit for your recovery, with her constant care at your bedside. Please remember me to her, Oliver, when you see her this evening."

He was patting my shoulder then, drawing me toward the door to ease my departure. I raised my hands. "On the matter that has brought me here, Dr. Ripple, will you allow me a few moments of your time?"

He came to a halt and struck his forehead. "Ah, yes, you spoke of it only moments ago, and already it has slipped my mind. *Tempus fugit*, Oliver, and along with it, one's claim to memory. Now, what is it that clouds your countenance so? We have dealt with your tonsils and eliminated that worry. Would it be the nagging cough of your uncle Rufus? Consumption is common here in Concord, my boy, and his condition, I assure you, is not yet of great concern."

I shook my head to this. "That is welcome news, sir, although I had not made the connection between his cough and the disease. I attributed it to the many cigars that he smokes. But I am aware of it, since Henry Thoreau tells me he expects to inherit the condition, and Mr. Emerson's brothers were afflicted gravely.

"I am here on other business. It concerns the death of the unfortunate woman you were called to attend at Walden Pond this morning. I wish to ascertain the circumstances, the manner, and the causes of her murder, as you found them."

He glanced sharply at me. "Are you here then for your journal, Oliver, to get the news for your uncle's readers?"

"That is part of it, sir," I replied. "But my interest and concern is far deeper. I have known Hetta Bird since my earliest days. As a child, I was terrified of her due to her strange attire and spirited ways. There were also the hearsay myths and frightening legends about her, adding to the superstitious fears of an impressionable young mind. But as I grew, I developed a fondness for her, one shared by my friends who also had harassed her with crude, childish pranks. That fondness has with time developed further to a genuine affection and pity for her condition.

"So I come here today to ascertain from you the manner of her death, how it was done, and to what extent the visible blow to her head contributed its fatal effect."

Dr. Ripple was nodding, attentive to my words. Then, abruptly, his hand grasped mine with a firmness unnatural to his years. His eyes were glowing with a fiery intensity. "Pray, be seated, Oliver. It should in no way surprise you to learn that I have known Hetta far longer than any in this village, and that affection you held for her was in no way greater than mine. Indeed, I was horrified beyond belief, despite my many years of viewing death, to witness her own."

My knees buckled at this revelation, and I sat limply, staring at him. A prickly awareness stirred my mind. Somehow I had always viewed Hetta as she was most recently, an old woman. Now here was Dr. Ripple with a better perspective.

"How was it then, sir, that you came to know her? Was it in her youth? And forgive my asking, but was the dear woman always so addled as to be thought mad?"

Dr. Ripple inhaled noisily through his nose, and his stern glance rebuked me. "No more odd or addled or even mad than yourself or me," he said. "I am past eighty now, and came here directly from my medical studies in Boston in my early twenties. Hetta was a child then, perhaps the same age as our Louisa May. Indeed, Hetta was my first case when I arrived here, still wet behind the ears, with no practical experience as a physician." He looked at the voluminous notebook, reached for it, and then withdrew his hand. "The incident is in there but needs no referral. It is as fresh in my mind still as if it happened yesterday."

My knees locked together of their own accord, as if aware by premonition of the dire revelation to come.

"Since she is past caring now of any violation of the trust between doctor and patient," I said, "I would most earnestly entreat you, sir, for the history of it. I give you my word it will go no further, but to know more of this unfortunate woman's early life would do me a distinct favor. Uncle Rufus has brought me up to detest one-sidedness, and yet that is all the picture I have of her."

Dr. Ripple sat nodding absently for a time, then rose and walked to his window. He stood there for a long moment, as if looking out, but I sensed a far longer view into the distant past. When he spoke, it was with a most profound melancholy, his thin voice hoarse with emotion.

"One-sidedness," he repeated. "You have chosen the correct word to apply to Hetta. One-sidedness is the history of Hetta Bird's life, and it was all one-sided against her. You sense the torment of her later years, but I can assure you that, in retrospect, they were by far the better ones.

"Her mother died of exposure one winter when Hetta was eleven. Hetta had no father, no kin, could not read or write her name. She was taken in by some alleged kind soul, was illtreated, made a slave, was starved and beaten until she rebelled and ran away. I gathered this three years later, when I met a destitute girl in the last throes of pregnancy."

Surprised, I asked, "Then she had a child?"

Dr. Ripple shook his head no. "True, I was inexperienced, but I believe I was not at fault. The infant was stillborn, already dead, with a deformity as well. Hetta seemed to take the tragedy calmly. You see, what had happened to her during those three years made everything that was to follow unimportant."

I sat with rigid attention, regretful of my need to know more. There was nothing in my experience to cope with the horrors the doctor was unraveling. Still, I could not let him stop at this point.

"Yours was perhaps the child's first experience with kindness," I said.

"I performed no kindness other than seeing to her needs," Ripple said. "But I must include what happened to Hetta prior to the pregnancy, if you are to understand what can drive certain of us to madness.

"A drover found her in the fields hiding from those she'd fled. On the pretext of helping her, he brought her to a hut in the woods. He held her captive there, bound and unable to leave, violating the child at his will. He then invited his friends and, later, strangers who would pay to have their pleasure. In time, he sold her to another rascal who continued this sordid entertainment."

His voice faltered, and I raised my hand. "Enough, Dr. Ripple," I cried. "There is no need to continue further. I can easily imagine the transition now from helpless degradation to madness."

"Not yet," he answered quickly. "One cannot recount such a history without its most egregious wrongs.

"Hetta tried to kill herself by whatever means. She ate some vermin poison and became violently ill. Her captor feared then for his own involvement and cast her into the woods. She crawled to the river and tried to drown herself. She was plucked from the water by a fisherman. He in turn thought he would have his way with her, but she began to cough blood. The lout was frightened then and brought her ashore. An Indian family of trappers found her, purged her, and saved her life. But they feared for their own involvement with her very serious condition and left her at the church."

Dr. Ripple stepped across the room then to lean toward me, his eyes intently scanning mine. "You would assume her troubles would have been over then, Oliver, but you would be wrong. In the end, before she was twenty, Hetta learned a marvelous protective device. She covered herself with filth and transported herself into madness."

I sat silent, stunned by this accounting. Images I held of myself and companions confronting the wraithlike woman of the woods whirled in my brain: her odd mutterings and imprecations when we teased and tormented her with our catcalls, her sudden mood changes and childlike swoops into song and dancing. They were all still present in my head, so many I became dizzy. And finally, at the end, the last meeting, wherein she pronounced her strange prophecy that was meant to include me but instead foretold her own death.

"How did she die then?" I asked. "Was it of the poisoned hemlock berries that Henry suggested, or the blow to her head?"

Dr. Ripple eyed me stonily. "It was neither, Oliver. The poor woman died of fright. It was simple heart failure."

"What? Are you quite certain?" I said.

He nodded. "After so many years of living inviolate, you might say, this sudden new assault proved too much for her. It was a ghostly reminder of the many times she had been brutalized earlier in her life. She had wished herself dead before, and I believe this time she welcomed and embraced it."

In Which Charley Bigbow
Provides Astounding Proof
of His Heritage

A brief return to my office at the *Concord Freeman* assured me that Uncle Rufus had sent no telegram about a further change in his plans regarding his stay in New York. There was nothing more I could do there of any use, as I was spent with emotion after Dr. Ripple's evocation of Hetta's early life. I tarried idly a while longer, in hopes for word from Charley Bigbow. There was nothing, and in truth I was in such great despair that dire news might be forthcoming that I bolted from the office and returned home.

Aunt Martha was pleased when I informed her that she might have an unexpected guest for dinner. "Charley Bigbow!" she exclaimed with a broad smile and widened, pleased eyes. "How wonderful! I haven't seen that young rascal for years. I do hope he comes."

"If he does, it will be after dark," I cautioned. "Charley is too aware of how some townspeople might take the sight of an Indian approaching a white house."

My gentle aunt Martha's eyes flashed, and her voice was as untempered as ever I had heard it. "You cannot mean that, Oliver. In this day and age?"

I shrugged. "Well, to our shame, it is the truth. He would not bring dishonor to your door."

Aunt Martha's mouth flew open in dismay. "Oliver, what are you saying? You are speaking of your dearest childhood friend, one I am most fond of." She looked at me suspiciously. "Surely you are joking."

"It is no joking matter, Aunt. Charley has even learned to speak a primitive English to ensure he won't be put in his place and perhaps be lynched."

She began to move pots about on the stove, handling them roughly. "Your uncle Rufus will hear of this, mark my word, on his return."

"What would Uncle Rufus do?" I asked.

"Do?" she exclaimed heatedly. "What would he do? Well, he has a newspaper, hasn't he? He says it's to educate the people and improve the culture, doesn't he? Well, let me tell you, sir, that Rufus Puckle will be devoting more of his precious space to the Indian account in the immediate future if he intends to share my home."

In all my years with her, it was the strongest statement I had ever heard Aunt Martha make. I looked at her with new appreciation. "How would you manage that, if Uncle refuses? Would you throw him out?" I added, amused.

Aunt Martha tossed her head with spirit. "There are ways, Oliver. Beyond your ken, perhaps, but there are ways."

"Name one," I said. "I am most eager to hear."

"He will find a cold supper and a colder bed," she said. "There, and you have my word on it."

She was so serious and stern, I had to laugh, and I hugged her. "No matter what, I am on your side, Aunt."

She patted my head. "The matter does not concern you, Oliver."

I shook my head in amusement and was saved from having to make any further response by a noise outside the back door. A soft sound, the mournful cry of a hooting owl. We have no nesting owls among our trees.

"That's Charley," I said.

To my surprise, Aunt Martha bustled past me through the kitchen and opened the back door. "Is that you, Charles Bigbow?" she asked.

I heard his soft reply. "Yes, Aunt Martha."

She surprised me again by saying, "I would greatly appreciate it, Charley, if you never used this door again. You will kindly go around to the front, where we receive our most respected friends."

There was a brief silence, and then Charley said from the darkness, "The trouble, Aunt Martha, is that I am not alone. I am here with a friend."

Aunt Martha opened the door wider, peering into the dark night. "Well then, bring him around with you."

"It is not a him, Aunt Martha," Charley said softly. "It is a her. Perhaps Oliver will assist me—"

I leaped past my aunt toward the door opening. For the moment, I saw nothing but the velvety darkness, and then, as my eyes adjusted, I could see the shadowy figure of Charley Bigbow close to the wall of the house.

"Charley, what is it?" I exclaimed. "Why don't you come inside?"

"I wanted to make sure, Oliver, that she is welcome. She claims to know you, and her name is Margaret Roberts," he said. He pulled her into the light. "She is most *alluring company*, Oliver. Perhaps you would prefer another—?"

In Which the Truth Is Disclosed Regarding the Disappearance of Margaret Roberts, Her Perilous Flight, and Rescue

The maiden who stepped inside in no way resembled the immaculate one who had visited my office. Her long blond hair was unkempt, matted, and disheveled. Her face was smeared with dirt. Her frock was torn and discolored with stains of various hues. Her arms were scratched and covered with welts and bruises. Her shoes were caked with mud and grass and berry stains.

Before I could utter a word of welcome and concern, my aunt had swooped between us, put a comforting arm around her shoulders, and led her away upstairs.

"Poor child," Aunt Martha said, "is this how they have treated you for associating with an Algonquin?" She turned her head to fix me with her eyes. "I trust this will remind you of our conversation earlier, Oliver. I will not have another instance of this here in Concord."

Charley gaped at me, as well he might have. "I never discussed the matter of the girl's disappearance with my aunt," I said, "so she has drawn her own conclusions." I informed him of the direction Aunt Martha's mind had suddenly taken. He leaned back against the wall, laughing.

"Mark my words," I said, "she will soon order heating for your wigwams."

"What's a wigwam?" Charley said.

We both laughed, and I threw my arm around his shoulders, unable to control my joy and relief. We stood looking at each other, both happy at whatever provenance had brought us together again.

"I don't know yet how you managed to find her," I said, "but I shall be eternally grateful."

"It was nothing really, Oliver," he said, his dark eyes dancing. "Just what the noble savage does best. Stalking silently, carefully noting the presence or displacement of every leaf and blade of grass. Scenting the air for the merest hint of a girl from Boston lost or murdered in our woods. Listening for the fluttering of her heartbeat, the soft sound of her falling tears, the echoes of her little feet."

"I am too happy to deny you your fun with me," I said. "I will not even criticize the Indian mating call you voiced outside to attract my attention."

"I don't do owls that well," Charley said. "I'm better at loons, but New England Indians mostly do owls. Anyway, the girl has not been hurt or harmed, as she will tell you herself when she has recovered. She has had a bad experience, a genuine fright. There is still the matter of her pursuer being at large, and that's why I brought her here for safekeeping, under cover of darkness."

"Then how and where did you find her?" I asked. "You may elaborate and make it as difficult as you like."

"Well, she was comparatively safe when I found her," he said. "The only dangers were the rotted potatoes, turnips, and beans that surrounded her in Henry's cellar."

"She was in Thoreau's hut?"

"She found the trapdoor to his rotting hoard of vegetables," Charley said, holding his nose. "He hates to throw anything away, you know. A most frugal man."

"Perhaps he hoards them for the runaway slaves that he shelters, Charley. Surely we can allow him that. But how did you track her to Thoreau's hut?"

"I asked myself where I would hide if I were a frightened girl being pursued through the woods. I saw the hut and climbed in through the side window."

"But why the window? Henry never locks his door."

Charley smiled mischievously. "That is what you might ask Miss Roberts."

"Are you saying she was there all the time we were outside looking at Hetta's body?"

"No, because she had found another place to hide then. She found Hetta's hut. That's never locked either, as you may recall."

I remembered the simple wooden latch Hetta had nailed to her door, and the equally primitive one inside. Hetta's hut was not far from Thoreau's. There was a winding path from the upper swampy area where Hetta lived down along to Walden Pond and the small shelter he had built. I could imagine the girl fleeing the one for the other, less secluded hut. Henry's door is always open, and he leaves a chair outside for visitors.

"But when did she go from one to the other?" I asked.

"Henry was in jail the night she disappeared," Charley said. "His hut was vacant then, and perhaps she chanced upon it while trying to elude her pursuer. It may be that she was hiding there this morning, but had collapsed under the strain, or was still fearful to appear. Or she might have slipped in this evening at dusk, since it is then Henry usually leaves for home and his mother's warm supper."

I shrugged, unable to choose between the two. "It is immaterial now that she is safe, and she will doubtless explain the details, Charley. What concerns me most now is how we will know the pursuer, who killed Hetta whether by chance or design."

"Well, I cannot help you there. Henry will point out the criminal, never fear."

"Henry?" I said, surprised. "How would he know? He was safely in jail during the time this happened."

"That is the puzzle exactly, Oliver. As a full-blooded Indian, I'm ashamed to say that Thoreau has an understanding of woodcraft superior to mine. He talks to these inanimate woods, you know, and for all I know, they answer."

Wherein Margaret Roberts Discloses the Unusual Circumstances That Decided Her to Leave Boston for Concord

In a little while, Aunt Martha came downstairs and walked directly to the kitchen. Charley and I looked in vain for the girl's appearance, and then to my aunt for explanation.

"She is exhausted and cannot join us now for supper," Aunt Martha said. "She is in the bath at the moment, and I will bring her a light broth later. I will feed you gentlemen now, and perhaps she will join us presently. Charley, do excuse me, as I had much to talk with you about. You are always most welcome here, and I hope you will visit with us again soon."

With that, she set our plates on the table and excused herself to return upstairs for further care of our unexpected guest.

As we fell to, Charley said musingly, "Either I've been away too long or your aunt has changed. I always thought of her as fluttery and kind, content to be a gracious listener. She seems more direct and formidable now."

"You are so right, Charley," I said. "You may not believe it, but the change has just occurred this evening, and you are the one responsible for it. When I told her you would be coming under cover of night so as to cause no outcry over an Indian visiting our house, she almost suffered a stroke of righteous indignation. She also made it clear that she expects her husband to take a strong editorial stand in the *Concord Freeman* concerning the town's attitude toward our native Indians."

Charley grinned and stuffed more of Aunt Martha's leg of lamb in his mouth. "What will your uncle have to say about this democratic nonsense?"

"I shudder to think of it," I said. "She is in a state of war frame of mind. He cannot hope to win her over and will concede, I think."

Charley's eyes flashed. "Your uncle has never been afraid to speak his mind. If he speaks now for us, he will have Emerson's support and Bronson Alcott's. I hope my father stays sober when I tell him."

We finished our plates and took them to the kitchen for rinsing. Charley admired the new stove Aunt Martha had installed recently. "You know," he said, "Henry still does his cooking outside, in a small hole dug in the earth, lined with stones. It is most efficient."

"What does he cook?" I asked.

"He has an odd diet," Charley said. "It is mostly rye and Indian meal. Potatoes, rice, and a little salt pork. He favors molasses, and water to drink. He has bread, butter, cheese, and popcorn. He has no head for liquor and detests tobacco, as you must already know."

"His distastes are contrary to mine," I said. "Let us sit in the parlor and enjoy some of the choice cigars my uncle Rufus always has on hand."

In our parlor Charley looked at the cigar I gave him with suspicion. "Are you certain your uncle smokes these in the house?"

"Well, of course," I said. "Why else are they here?"

Charley shook his head. "Mr. Emerson does not enjoy such privilege," he said. "He smokes outside on his walks, and is most careful to deposit the stub of what remains on the post outside the door before reentering."

We laughed at the restriction suffered by our leading citizen.

"Well, Henry's father is permitted to smoke in his workshop outside the house," I said.

"Hawthorne did his puffing in the taverns," Charley said. "Bronson Alcott does not smoke, does he?"

"It would offend Bronson to harm a tobacco leaf with fire," I said. "No, he rules his household like no other. Abba Alcott is far too compliant, to my mind."

Charley blew smoke away, shaking his dark head. "I cannot imagine how she allows her husband to weave and cut the garments for his daughters to wear. Does she not see they look like ghosts trailing their loose sheets? Even more surprising to me is Louisa May being party to his notions of fashion for young girls."

"Give her time," I said. "I spoke with her yesterday, and she is on the brink. She is aware and ashamed, Charley, and that is the first step."

Charley nodded. "The only fault I find with Louisa May is her adoration for Henry. Is it because she was his pupil, do you think, for the brief time before he retired himself from the profession?"

"I can think of no other reason," I said pettily.

We turned from gossip then to memories of our childhood, each instance suggesting another. How we had worked together one summer at the Middlesex Hotel and had innocently ruined the dinners for a group from Boston seeking the acclaimed pleasures of my uncle Barnaby's kitchen. He had set Charley and me to work scouring the pots and preparing the vegetables. We had soaped the pots but neglected to rinse them thoroughly. The hurried departure from the dining room tables of guests, grimacing with bubbly mouths and clutching their stomachs, was a scene never to be forgotten.

We regaled each other with other incidents we had shared through the years, at school or at play. It was inevitable that in this vein of recollection our earliest encounters with Hetta Bird would come to mind. Suddenly our lips were stilled as conscience and guilt combined to bring us sorrowfully to the present.

"Who could have done it?" I cried. "Why must we wait for Henry Thoreau to lead us to the killer?"

"Perhaps I can assist you there," a soft voice said. "It is partly my doing."

Charley and I leaped to our feet. Miss Roberts had her wet hair done up in a towel. Her face was freshly scrubbed to a silken, radiant pink, and she was lost in the voluminous folds of my aunt's bathrobe and the house slippers of my uncle. She looked to be recovered from her ordeal, but both Charley and I outdid ourselves in solicitously urging her to sit and rest.

"I will sit," she said, "but shall not rest until you both have heard my story. I have brought you two into extreme jeopardy due to my willfulness and must explain truthfully why I have come to Concord."

Charley and I looked at each other uncomfortably, holding our half-smoked cigars. She noticed and smiled. "Do continue with your smoking," she said. "I love the aroma of good tobacco." She wrinkled her nose. "Indeed, I welcome it now, as my nostrils are still filled with the noxious odors of parsnips, turnips, and rotted potatoes."

"Your mistake was in choosing the trapdoor to Henry's cellar," Charley said. "His garret would have been a far better choice."

"It can be reached by stepping on the chair," I said.

She smiled. "I wanted a place to hide. The trapdoor to a cellar seemed ideal. How was I to know the man was so enamored of old vegetables?"

"He grows them as a means of survival so that he might concentrate on his writing," I said. "But you need not have crawled through his window to enter. Thoreau's door is never locked."

"There is a chair outside for visitors," Charley said. "You could have sat and watched the setting sun."

She looked at us and smiled. "It's a pity you two were not along. I could have used such cheer and good advice."

"You did well enough in your instinctive way to survive," I

said. "Do not mistake our comments for lack of concern or belittlement of your ordeal. We are only making light of it to help you forget a most frightening episode."

"I understand and am most appreciative," she said. "And if it were not for your Indian friend finding me with his remarkable instinct, I might still be there."

She paused and stared into the distance a moment, seeming to collect herself. Then she smiled at us again and said she would begin her story.

"Five years ago, my dearest friend, Mary Rogers, was murdered. There was evidence that she had been assaulted, strangled, and then drowned. The incident was in all the city newspapers. Do you recall it?"

We shook our heads. "I was not then in news gathering. Perhaps my uncle will remember on his return."

She shrugged. "It does not matter. What is more important is that the newspapers periodically reviewed the story, inasmuch as it was a sensational unsolved case. But this meant that I was never allowed to forget what had occurred, and I felt the urge to somehow bring her murderer to justice."

She looked at me. "Do you know of Mr. Edgar Allan Poe, the poet and writer?"

"Indeed I am most aware and respectful of his work," I said, happy to know that she was acquainted with the contemporary world of letters.

"Well, Mr. Poe was dissatisfied with the clumsy solutions offered by the crime analysts," she said. "He professed to have solved the matter himself, and indeed wrote of it in his story entitled 'The Mystery of Marie Rogêt.' Have you read that, Mr. Puckle?"

"Alas, no," I said. "I have read his earlier one, 'The Murders in the Rue Morgue.' His detective, the Chevalier C. Auguste Dupin, was a brilliantly conceived character, I thought."

She tossed her head in disdain. "Well, I have read it, and thought his solution shallow and spurious."

I murmured my objection with care. "One is at risk questioning the deductive powers of Mr. Poe," I said. "Do you recall his solution?"

"He deduced it was a visiting seaman. He offered the peculiar knot used in the strangulation of my friend. A knot common to seafaring men, said Mr. Poe."

"And you found that inconclusive?" I asked.

"Indeed," she replied. "It is the same sort of knot I use myself tying up a parcel, and I have never been to sea."

I looked to Charley, who shook his head mutely, venturing nothing. But the gleam in his eyes suggested his growing interest in the girl's story.

She then launched into the detailed accounting of it. I sat so absorbed in her rapt expression as she spoke that I could not follow her words closely enough.

Both she and the unfortunate Mary Rogers had lived on the same street in New York City and were as close as sisters. Mary Rogers lived with her widowed mother and worked as a cigar store clerk in the downtown business area. Margaret Roberts was employed close by in a millinery shop. The girls looked so much alike as to be thought sisters or twins.

Mary Rogers had told Margaret of a new customer from out of the city who had become infatuated with her. He had persisted in asking her out for an evening's entertainment. She kept putting it off, as he was a much older man. He continued in his visits and attentions, and eventually she agreed to join him on a weekend holiday boat trip. She met her death on that trip in a most brutal fashion, the body discovered later by some local people near the shore.

"She never divulged his name, not even a description of him," Margaret told us. "All I knew of him was that he was an older man, liked good cigars, and lived somewhere outside New York City."

Brokenhearted over the loss of her dearest friend, Margaret Roberts left her home and moved to Boston. There, on an impulse, she secured work as a clerk in a cigar store similar to that of her friend. She thought that perhaps one day this man would enter her store, and she by chance or intuition would recognize him.

"Intuition?" Charley interrupted. "Since you had never seen him, or had him described, how would you know him?"

"I was so close to Mary," the girl explained. "Our thoughts were so much alike. It seemed possible to me that, if I saw him, my heart would respond as hers did."

Charley scowled. "With such reasoning, it's no wonder you picked a cellar of rotted produce to fall in."

Margaret laughed quietly. "Yes," she said, "it was indeed a strange assumption. But then, you see, it did happen. The man came into the store, and I knew him immediately."

"*How* did you know him?" Charley persisted. "Did your heart roll over and tap out his name?"

Margaret regarded him patiently, without resentment. "It signaled something I could not identify. A feeling of dread, a prickling of my senses. But more to the point, he reacted with a start, as if *he* knew *me*.

"Remember," she continued, "Mary and I looked very much alike. He saw me, became flustered, and left the shop without giving his order."

Charley leaned forward, smiling, and spoke mockingly. "I know! I have read such stories. He recoiled upon seeing the ghost of the person he had ravished."

The girl nodded. "Exactly," she said.

I remembered my uncle Barnaby reminding me that women exercise a different kind of logic than men. Therefore, when I sensed Charley was about to assail her with more of his raking wit, I signaled him to silence. Prepared then as I was by Barnaby's admonition, I did not react visibly as Margaret recited her next venturesome move.

She quickly asked permission from her superior to leave the store and followed this customer. He went straightaway to the railroad station nearby and bought a ticket. When he proceeded to the platform, she ascertained from the ticket seller, on some pretext, the man's destination. Concord, she was told, and she returned to her place of employment.

She asked her fellow employees then if anybody knew his name. It appeared that nobody did, but it was known that he was a regular customer, coming to this store every month for another box of his brand of imported cigars. She waited for his next arrival, but when he failed to return, she surmised he hadn't because of her remindful presence. She then conceived her plan to arrive here in Concord on the odd chance of their meeting again. She would know him now, and he might again react upon seeing her.

She had known what her friend Mary had been wearing at the time of her unfortunate holiday cruise. Indeed, from her own millinery shop, she had prepared the special hats Mary Rogers wore. And, she added, even if she had forgotten, the numerous newspaper articles about Mary's sensational murder had described over and again the garments of the victim. Miss Roberts had ample time to prepare her own garments to correspond exactly. There were several of these, she said, in the suitcase she had left at Concord station—duplications of what Mary Rogers wore on that fateful day.

"Well, then I arrived, and you know the rest," she said, and sat back.

Charley and I exchanged baffled glances, shifted our eyes to her, and received no further explanation. The matter was already resolved in her mind.

Charley was the first to test this resolution. "We can discuss the logic of this later, if you like. But there remains a large gap between your arrival at Oliver's office and your situation among Thoreau's old vegetables. When and where and exactly how did this murderous chase begin?"

Before Margaret could answer, I interrupted. "There is another matter of more immediate concern. You may not know of this, but there was another woman found murdered at the Thoreau hut, in your stead."

"A dear, sweet old woman the village of Concord loved intensely," Charley said. "Whose departure from the living has left us all disconsolate."

The girl's eyes opened in horror. "I knew nothing of this, nor of the person to whom you refer!"

"Her name was Hetta Bird," I said. "She was found strangled perhaps near Walden Pond, and at her side was your parasol."

"Oh," she said. "I lost that in a thicket when I was running in fright." She thought a moment. "I lost my hat some time later, I think."

"Charley has recovered your hat," I said. "Your parasol would be in our sheriff's office and, after careful examination, will be returned to you. But try to remember the sequence. I saw you last heading to the Thoreaus' house. What happened to divert your intention?"

She replied that, since it was a lovely day and still early, she wanted to stroll through the woods. She had never before seen such an inviting forest available, and thought that the serene setting might focus her mind on the task at hand. There would be time enough to make her arrangement with Mrs. Thoreau. She thought, too, that, after a brief acquaintance with the woods, there would be time to casually walk the village and become familiar with its shape and features. Remembering what I had told her of the many women in the Thoreaus' house adept at conversation, she decided that, once inside, she would lose this first opportunity to be alone with her thoughts about how to best attract the attention of the man she suspected.

"So I walked from path to path," she said, "going ever deeper into the forest, loving the smells and quiet, the calls of the birds. After a while, I sat under a tree to rest. I closed my eyes, and to my surprise, when I opened them, it was dusk. I tried to hurry back the way I had come but instead got in deeper and deeper, soon realizing I was quite lost."

It was at this point that she became aware she was being followed. At first she believed her pursuer might be attempting to help her find her way, but when she stopped, the footfalls behind her stopped as well. When she called out, there was no answer. Thus she resumed her search for the way out, becoming more agitated and frightened as she fell into thickets that barred her path, ever more conscious of the relentless progress of the person following her.

At one point, she said, she was thoroughly startled and feared for her life. "An old scarecrow of a woman suddenly came at me from the bushes, flailing her arms and screaming horrible imprecations. I tripped and fell, and saw her pass by through the trees, alternating between screams and song."

"That was our dear Hetta," Charley said. "She was the one found murdered the next morning."

Miss Roberts shook her head. "I'm so terribly sorry, but she seemed quite mad. And her dress was remindful of a scarecrow."

"Hetta cared not for fashion," I said. "And the little hut you found next to hide in was her home."

Margaret looked at me in great surprise. "How do you come to know I hid there first?"

"Charley tracked you there," I said, "and later, in his redoubtable way, picked up your trail to the window, trapdoor, and cellar of our Henry Thoreau."

The girl looked at Charley with sparkling eyes and rapt expression. "How ever did you manage that?"

Charley thumped his chest. "Me Indian," he said. "You lost. Me find. Indian see everything. Better than bloodhound, who only smell."

Margaret laughed at his speech. "Then where were you when that man attacked me, trying to strangle me from behind? It was only my parasol that saved me. I struck him with it and managed to break his hold and escape."

"Indian not perfect," Charley said. "Only owl see so good at night."

"Did you manage to see his face?" I asked eagerly. "Was it the same man you saw in Boston?"

The girl shook her head. "It was too dark to see. He never spoke, so I don't know his voice. I think he was a large and clumsy man, as I eluded him quite easily."

"Well then," Charley said, "could you describe the man who came to your store in Boston?"

"No," she said. "It was merely a glance. There is nothing I remember of him. But I'm certain I would recognize him if we meet again."

"Miss Roberts," I said, "please attend these words of caution. You have no proof that the man who took your friend on the cruise was her murderer. You have no way of identifying the man from Boston, nor can you prove he was the man who enticed her in New York City. Whatever did you hope to accomplish by coming here?"

She raised her head at that, addressing me in a most calm and yet assured manner. "I am certain he will recognize me first. I came here wearing what my dear friend wore. When I meet the man who reacts with alarm to my presence, then I will know him."

"In the same manner you knew the man you said assaulted you in our woods?" Charley said.

"Nevertheless, he must have known me," she replied, frowning. "When we meet again, I shall accuse him of his crime. When he shows his guilt, I will demand his confession. I will then inform the proper local authorities."

I thought for a long moment, then said, "It is a most venturesome notion, Miss Roberts."

"Perhaps the murderer will throw himself to his knees," Charley said, "and beg forgiveness."

I reached across the low table for my uncle's brass humidor, extracted two fresh cigars, and gave one to Charley. "Your people make a big ceremony of smoking on this or that matter," I said. "Light up, my friend, while we deliberate."

"I think this is a more complicated affair," he said. "More likely a matter for the drinking ceremony."

His head inclined toward the decanter of wine on the nearby cabinet shelf. I brought it back with three glasses and filled them all.

Lifting mine, I said, "To your continuing health, Miss Roberts."

"I'll toss this down fast," Charley said. "My head is too clear and in need of more fuzziness."

Miss Roberts lifted her glass to ours, laughing. "After he confesses, I believe I shall stay on here in Concord. You two are more fun than anyone in Boston."

In Which Thoreau Redeems Himself by the Curious Process of Observation and a Relentless Memory

Early Sunday morning, I left the house determined to see Thoreau and extract from him whatever new sense he could make of Hetta's murderer. If indeed he chanced to be the same man Margaret Roberts was pursuing, she would be less at risk the sooner he was apprehended. The fantastical manner in which she presumed to determine his guilt was not only laughable but far too dangerous to permit.

The shops on the village square were closed, and I appeared to be the only one walking about at this early hour.

It was a bright, clear morning, the air bracing and refreshing. Down the long, sloping hillside was the pond, placid and serene, the morning wind scarcely stirring its smooth surface. The arrowy pines on the opposite side were still mist-covered, shadowy and majestic. A loon called in the distance, flapping its wings. Closer to the near side, a muskrat bobbed to the surface and paddled slowly to its burrow.

There was something so comforting in this immense soli-
tude that it conveyed a sense of the spiritual, and for the first
time, I could understand and appreciate why Thoreau had
built his tiny shingled and plastered house here. Most of the
original lot of eleven acres has been sold off, the pines and
hickories worth no more than eight dollars and eight cents
an acre. Thoreau has planted the remaining two and a half
acres of light, sandy soil with beans, chiefly, and added potatoes, corn, peas, and turnips. He told me once that the entire
income from his farm was less than $9.00. His accounting for
food eaten came to $8.74, he admitted, laughing, which proved
what he always knew, that he was not meant to be a businessman.

I have conducted short interviews with him in the past, never
at great length, as I still am not fully comfortable in his presence. He wears his learning lightly, although it is said he is at
ease in six languages, including ancient Greek and Latin. Mostly
he speaks in long and ponderous sentences that seem to never
end, each new phrase suggesting another. He was educated at
Harvard, at the considerable cost of $50 tuition and $188 for
room and board, yet he seems to ignore this investment in his
education, living like the most impoverished settler in his little
sentry box facing Walden Pond.

As I approached Thoreau's hut, I saw he was already there,
busily engaged with his surveying instruments and a length of
tape. His green-and-blue-painted boat was drawn up on the
ground.

When I came closer and bent to see what he was doing,

Thoreau looked up at me and smiled. "Good morning to you, sir," I said, and his smile widened.

"It was formerly the custom in our village," he said, "when a poor debtor came out of jail, for his acquaintances to salute him, looking through their fingers, which were crossed to represent the grating of a jail window, and say 'How do ye do?' "

"Old customs do not concern me, as most are silly," I said. "Are you always here so early at your work?"

He nodded, with a flick of his head toward the weak rising sun. "In any weather, at any hour of the day or night, I have been anxious to improve the nick of time, and notch it on my stick, too; to stand on the meeting of two eternities, the past and future, which is precisely the present moment; to toe that line."

"You shall be a model for me then, if ever I can develop your faultless character. But it is on the matter of the two eternities that I am here. I have been to Dr. Ripple, anxious to obtain the exact reason for Hetta's death. While he did not dismiss your notion of the poisoned hemlock berries, he likewise ignored the more obvious blow to her head, and he put it more simply by stating Hetta died of her fright and consequent heart failure."

Thoreau accepted my statement without embarrassment or argument. He said Dr. Ripple's judgment was usually sound, and that, as the doctor was neither a businessman nor a politician, he was one of the rare few worthy of respect in the town.

Still, Thoreau's theory of the forcible use of the berry intrigued me, even if it had not proved entirely accurate. What kind of murderer was this, intent upon poisoning first, then strangulation, and finally a blow to the head? Was this lengthy sequence due to inefficiency, as it seemed, or perhaps inexperience in completing the deadly act? I knew little of the mind of a murderer. There had been murders before in Concord, but they all seemed simple and direct affairs of sudden violence done in haste. Some were carried out in the heat of an argument, or in revenge for a fancied slight or wrong.

What had Hetta to do with this? Was it possible she had been the intended victim all along, or had the murderer mistaken her for Margaret Roberts because in the darkness he drew the wrong conclusion from the parasol Margaret had lost and Hetta found? Thoreau, with his analytical mind, was my only hope to provide the answer, I thought.

He rose to his feet then and pointed to the pond. "Your report on Dr. Ripple's notion of the actual cause of Hetta's death is a relief to my mind, as I was in error. I had wrongly assumed her attacker had carried her here. I see now that she had been running in fright, and when he overtook her, she collapsed in fear and died."

"Is this another assumption based on the weakness of her heart?" I asked.

He shrugged, staring at the ground. "The actual details do not matter now," he said, "as you will be more concerned, and properly so, with apprehending her assailant. Fortunately, I can help you there.

"I have retraced his path through these woods and examined his footprints and a spot where he hid himself. His footprints tell me two things." Thoreau cut off a short piece from the length of string he was holding. "There is the length of his stride. And he will be limping off his left foot. From his footprints I can see his heel there has come loose. An examination of the thicket where he lay in wait for his victim was likewise productive. He is a smoker of strong West Indian cigars. He is clumsy and large of stature. And you will find him for sure because of the sumac."

I stared at the string I now held tightly in my hands. "The sumac? Now you are basing conclusions about this criminal on another plant?"

Thoreau leaned closer to me, his large eyes so strangely tinted between blue and gray. "He chose a stand of poison sumac for his hiding place. He will have developed a severe rash by now. His face will be red and mottled, perhaps swollen. There well may be scratches on it from Hetta's long nails. He will most likely need immediate relief for his persistent itch. I suggest you inquire at our apothecary to learn what new customer is in need of salve and ointment."

"I will do as you suggest," I said warmly. "It is most remarkable, this genius you have for observation. In another time and age, you might have been burned as a witch."

He smiled. "Man will always be the victim of circumstances," he said.

I thanked him, adding, "There may be a reward for you if what you have adduced proves correct, Henry."

He allowed the familiar usage of his name now without notice. "It is all business and money here," he said. "Do you know it is far easier to find a book ruled for accounts and transactions than one for writing?"

Leaving him then, I returned to the village. As I passed the railroad, dotted with the clustered shanties, I could see the front doors open to admit the sun, the poor wretches huddled inside their miserable hovels, children playing on the earthen floors.

The village green was coming awake to the new day. Citizens were opening their doors, sweeping away leaves. As I came to Reynolds's apothecary shop, the door opened and a man stepped out. It was Gordon Goodfellow.

My face hardened as I saw him. He noticed my approach and offered a frosty nod of recognition. His hat was pulled low over his eyes, but I could see the reddened swelling and mottled skin. He tilted the long cigar in his mouth, turned, and limped away.

A limp, a cigar, the rash of the sumac! My heart sang! With difficulty, I persuaded myself not to trail after him and measure his stride with Thoreau's string.

Mr. Arthur Reynolds smiled, shaking his head, when I entered. "I'm sorry, Oliver," he said. "But if you have come back to resume your old job of delivery boy, the position has been long filled."

"I'm here on another matter, Mr. Reynolds," I said. "But I do remember fondly my employ here. You were always most tolerant of the many vials and nostrums I dropped and broke hurrying to ease those emergency cases."

"I did the same when I was a lad," he said, nodding with affection as we shook hands. "I trust your uncle Rufus has increased your salary and lessened your work hours."

"Some of the former and less of the other," I said. I looked at the shelves behind him. "I've been careless passing the sumac in the woods. Do you have anything to prevent the sting and itch?"

His eyebrows wriggled, and he wagged his gray head. "Why, what a coincidence!" he exclaimed. "Mr. Goodfellow was just in with a similar complaint. But I am surprised in your instance, Oliver, as you were raised in our woods."

"I was careless, and in a hurry," I said. "It was moments ago, visiting Thoreau."

"There is no excuse for being careless with those poisonous plants," Mr. Reynolds said severely. He turned to busy himself with the ointments and bottles for the affliction, which still stood exactly where I remembered seeing them years before.

"Was Mr. Goodfellow also afflicted with the sumac?" I asked.

"He could not say, unfamiliar as he is with the natural world. His skin was scratched as well, leaving him more vulnerable to the plant secretions, so I gave him something that covers all similar rashes. Since you have just come from there, perhaps a milder formula will do you. Wash the area with strong soap first. If it worsens, I suggest your seeing Dr. Ripple, who may suggest another ointment."

He handed me the jar, waving his hands and refusing payment. "I would as soon charge my son, if I had one, Oliver. Go in health, and remember me to Rufus and Martha."

In Which Sheriff Staples Considers the Arrest of a Leading Citizen

The jailhouse was quiet in the morning. The prisoners had been let out to work in the fields and repay their debt to society in that fashion. When I arrived, Sheriff Staples admitted me, puffing on his pipe, jovial and good-humored as usual at the start of his day.

"If you have come for news regarding Hetta's killer, I have made no progress in the matter," he said. "Charley Bigbow has informed me that the missing Miss Roberts has been assisted to safety." He waved his pipe at me in a smiling, indulgent way. "I expect you already know that."

"Yes, and she is in the care of Aunt Martha," I said. "But I am here today not to gather news but to offer some you may be interested to hear."

"Wal, I vum!" he said. "Another killing? They do come in pairs, it happens."

"No, but rather bearing on the one concerning Hetta. Sam,

you told me your time was up here, and you were being asked to retire soon. Let me ask you this. If you were offered a renewal of your contract, would you stay on as sheriff?"

His expression remained bland, but his yellow eyes squinted into mine. "You are developing a certain cunning to your ways, Oliver, I notice, as you get older. To answer your question, of course I would stay on, but there is no chance of it. The board of selectmen gives the order."

"Well then, what if you were to solve this case and bring the murderer to justice, would you not then be regarded as a hero and begged to stay?"

Staples laughed. "A hero, you're saying? Well, no chance of that here in Concord. As to the rest of it, no doubt they would reconsider and let me stay on."

"Good," I said, holding the bit of string before his eyes. "Keep this while I tell you what I know."

We sat on opposite sides of his desk, and he heard without interruption what I had gathered from Thoreau. I concluded with my visit to the apothecary of Mr. Reynolds and produced, with a dramatic flourish, the jar of ointment Mr. Reynolds had given me, setting it triumphantly upon the sherff's desk. It was only then that I noticed he had become so absorbed in my story that he was tying knots in the string with which Thoreau had estimated.

"There you have it," I proclaimed vigorously. "The murderer of Hetta Bird!"

"Goodfellow?" Staples said. "He runs the board of selectmen. He is the one who has given me notice."

"Nevertheless, he is your man," I said.

"But you have offered me no proof," he said. He dropped the string on his desk. "You need evidence to convict a man of murder, Oliver. Surely you must have learned that from your uncle. This is fine, all you have told me, but what is needed is a witness to the crime itself, you see. *That* is evidence."

"Surely it is enough to take him in for questioning," I said.

"Oliver," Staples said, "you know this town and how it is run. Gordon Goodfellow is not only one of our town selectmen, he is also the owner of our biggest bank."

"Sumac does not grow in banks," I said. "His itch and rash are evidence that he was there in the woods."

"It may prove he was in the woods," Staples growled, "but the rash will not tell you what time he was there to get it. Nor is it evidence that he killed Hetta. What's the matter with you, boy? Have you lost your senses? I'm angry, too, over Hetta's murder, but still, it must be done all proper and legal. Not only would Goodfellow make me look stupid, but I'd be laughed out of town. Show me proof he did it, Oliver, is what I'm saying."

He was right, of course, and I was stunned over my lack of reasoning. Still, I could not let Goodfellow off the hook, and in desperation I thought of the girl.

"What if it could be proved that he murdered a girl in New York City a few years ago? Would that interest you?"

Staples stared at me and scratched his head. "Well, New York City is out of my jurisdiction, Oliver, and I don't see the connection. What's that about?"

"It concerns the girl Margaret Roberts, who was lost

overnight in the woods. She was attacked by a mysterious man there but escaped. It was her parasol Hetta picked up, flaunted, and was killed for, by mistake, you see. Miss Roberts followed a man here from Boston, in the belief that he killed her friend in New York City. She believes she can identify him."

Staples shook his head, set his pipe down, and picked up another. "Most interesting, Oliver. Did your Miss Roberts see the man kill her friend? I'm saying, can she prove it beyond doubt?"

It was the same weak link that had bothered me, and Staples was right if he thought me an imbecile. "Her thought is that since she and her murdered friend look alike, if she confronts the suspected man, he will give himself away, although she admits she cannot describe the man and is here solely driven by her intuition."

Staples shrugged, looking dour. "It's a fine thing, the intuition of women, but I'd not wish to be hanged by it, and I vum neither would you."

I looked at him, crestfallen. "Then you can do nothing?"

"Well, that's about all I've heard so far, Oliver. A lot of nothing. If you want me to hold Goodfellow on suspicion of murder, you'll have to do better by far, and show me proof."

With that, he got to his feet and stretched, and I knew that, despite Thoreau's remarkable clues, I had failed, not only to convince Staples but to convince myself as well.

As I turned to leave, he said in good nature, "I'll make it simple for you, Oliver. Find me a witness who was at the scene of the crime and saw it happen."

In Which Charley Bigbow Succeeds
by Sheer Luck Where the Narrator
Has Failed by Diligence

The need for proper evidence against Goodfellow occupied my mind as I walked through the village. Soon I was at the railroad station. The baggage master permitted me to secure the suitcase Margaret Roberts had left there on her arrival, and I took it home with me, hoping to surprise her with my thoughtfulness.

Aunt Martha took it, explaining the girl was still in bed, exhausted from her perils of the day before. The ointment from the pharmacist was my next offering, and my aunt, knowing of its efficacy, was pleased.

"Why, Oliver, that is most kind and thoughtful of you," she said. "She is a sweet girl and will be most appreciative if indeed she has contracted sumac poisoning."

"It was no trouble, Aunt," I said. "I was passing by."

She then waved a telegram at me. "Your uncle will be returning by late stage today. Are you all caught up with your work for the paper?"

"I'm on my way there now, Aunt," I said. "There are still some scraps to finish."

There was little more I could do now, since the sensational news I had hoped for, finding Hetta's killer, was still in doubt. I was happy to see Charley Bigbow waiting outside the paper's premises, as we had much to talk about.

As we walked to my desk, Charley said, "He wasn't at church today. Do you think the guilt was too much for him to attend?"

"Goodfellow?" I laughed and told him of what had happened at the apothecary. "Since when have you been going to church, Charley?"

"Since I suspected Goodfellow," he said. "I did my observing outside."

"I was busy, too," I said.

"I know. I saw you go to the jail. What was that about?"

"If I tell you," I countered, "you must tell me why you suspect Goodfellow, too."

He listened with interest as I told of my visit with Thoreau, the unusual hints he had given me, and Sheriff Staples's disposal of them. I added the possible contribution of Margaret Roberts and her intuitive bent, and what Staples thought of that.

"It's reassuring to know our sheriff is in favor of the legal process," Charley said. "Maybe I won't get lynched here after all."

"If you were, I would write a strong editorial on it, Charley, condemning the lynching party."

"I appreciate that, Oliver. But now that I've met Margaret

Roberts, I prefer being alive. Does she remember more today of her phantom assailant?"

"She is still resting. I doubt that she could identify him. It was too dark. Yet I thought Thoreau's suggestions were somehow incriminating."

"Only if the villain incriminated himself," he said. "The itch is not uncommon, the limp hardly suspect, and a man is not likely to return to the scene to search for a cast heel."

I nodded in agreement. "It is a waste," I said, "that we cannot make better use of Henry's calculations."

Charley was grinning. "Brace yourself, Oliver. I have gone back through the woods and have done far better than Mr. Thoreau."

"The last you spoke of this," I said, "you were repining over his superiority to your own woodcraft."

"Yes," he acknowledged, "but this morning, I was lucky. Look at this."

With a grand flourish, Charley took from his pocket a gleaming object and placed it on my desk.

"What is this?" I asked.

"Goodfellow's pocket watch. His engraved initials are on the back casing."

Attached to the stem of the embossed gold watch was a long pocket chain of gold. I turned the watch over and saw clearly the ornate initials, G.G. When I snapped the case open, the handsome face was revealed to show delicately cut hands and elegant numerals. It was an expensive timepiece such as only the wealthy wore inside their vests. A man would not suffer to lose such a watch, I thought, if it could be found again even with some effort.

I leaped to my feet with renewed hope. "Come on, Charley, and show Sam Staples your find. He laughed at me before, but he will not this time, I promise. It may very well serve as our missing witness."

With that, I locked the door of the *Concord Freeman* and we dashed across the road. "Where did you find it?" I asked as we ran.

"In the poison sumac patch uphill from Thoreau's hut," he said. "Perhaps the chain came loose and he lost it when he struggled with Miss Roberts."

"Then you believe her story?"

"If it proves true," he said, "I will apologize later."

In Which the Search for
the Foul Miscreant Is Concluded
and Justice Done

There was no agreement among us about when he would come. There was as well the possibility that he would not, or not on this night, at least. But Sheriff Staples and I waited in hope, huddled inside Thoreau's little house, staring out into the blackness of the night through the open door, our ears sharply attentive to any furtive sound.

And of sounds there were many, sharply distinct and pleasing to us townspeople. There were the hooting of owls, the fluting of wood thrush, the glurping of frogs, and the piercing screams of the diving fish hawk selecting his kill in Walden Pond.

Then another shrill sound, the long-drawn whistle of the locomotive carrying its cars and freight along to Boston from the north and west, its cloud of steam billowing into the sky, the iron wheels clanking their own discordant harmonies.

There was a soft whistle, and Charley Bigbow stuck his head in the doorway. He was panting from his run.

"He is on his way," he whispered. "He will be on the path cutting around the house, coming down from the blackberry and huckleberry patch. He is wearing white gloves and carrying a lantern, and you would be blind to miss him."

With this admonition, he slipped out the door and disappeared silently into the night.

"It suits Charley to be an Indian only when he pleases," I muttered.

"I'll give him his due if this works," Sheriff Staples whispered.

"It will work," I said confidently, "and I promise you a hero's headline in next week's paper."

"Hero be damned," Staples said. "I'm more worried about what Thoreau will say if he catches me using his house as a cover."

"I explained the need, Sam," I said, "and he voiced no objection. If it proves to be Goodfellow, Henry will be relieved at last of a long-standing grudge. The man cost him his teaching position, you may remember."

"Well, the truth is, nobody likes Goodfellow anyway," Staples said. "There are cheers waiting for us all in this. I'm not sure we should have put the girl in it. Seems risky."

"She liked the idea, Sam," I said. "It's her own notion to prove something that started all this."

"Sounds plumb crazy," Staples said. "Coming all this way without no stitch of proof."

It had been a long time since I had been inside Thoreau's house in the woods, and I found myself taking an inventory of his meager furnishings. He has always said that we all accumulate more than we need, and that any man with sense could make do with far less. Indeed the proof was there.

Beside the bed was a table, a desk, three chairs, and a small looking glass three inches wide. There were a pair of tongs, andirons, a kettle, a skillet, and a frypan. There was a dipper and a washbowl. Two knives and forks. Three plates, one cup, one spoon. A jug of oil, a jug for molasses, and a japanned lamp. There was his spyglass on the desk for sighting birds.

I picked up the spyglass and sighted through the side window. Far up the blackberry patch, I saw the weaving light of the lantern. With excitement barely contained, I so informed the sheriff, who nodded.

"The glass puts him closer, Oliver. Stay calm," he said softly.

The moon came out from behind drifting clouds. The entire clearing, from Thoreau's hut to the shore of Walden Pond, suddenly became bathed in light, the stumps of trees he had cut casting strong shadows. An owl hooted nearby and then closer still. Charley was getting better at it, I thought, with practice.

The lantern and the man came into view then, and it was plainly Gordon Goodfellow, stooping to peer into the thickets of berries, dropping to his knees at times to paw at the tangled roots. Then he came around the side of the house, walking slowly and peering carefully among the scattered stumps.

Sheriff Staples stepped out of the hut and walked slowly toward the stooped-over man. "Well, good evening to you, Mr. Goodfellow," he said. "Fine night for berry picking, is it not?"

Goodfellow jerked up, spinning around. "What? Who's there? Is that you, Sam?" He peered shortsightedly, lifting his lantern. "What? Yes, yes, a good night for picking berries."

Staples walked closer. "Wal, I vum, you've come without your bucket, it seems. How do you do it then, stuff your pockets with them?"

Goodfellow set his glowing lantern down to face Staples squarely. "What sorts of questions are these, Sam?" he said, bristling. "A citizen is free to walk where he pleases, I believe, without your concern."

"True enough," Staples said. "But it's an odd time to do the walking. Close to midnight, it is, as you would know if you looked at your watch."

Goodfellow's hand retreated to his vest pocket and then fell away. "What difference does it make what time it is? It's a pleasant night, and I thought a walk in the woods would help my sleep."

Staples nodded agreeably. "Nothing wrong with that, either, Mr. Goodfellow. But a good walk is more agreeable along the shore of the pond than among the berry patches. There's a lack of the good night air up in the thickets."

"Uh . . . well, yes, you have a point there, Sam. The truth of it is, I've lost something and come back to look for it here, you see."

"Well now, that makes more sense," Staples said. "What was it you lost?" He waved toward me as I came out of the hut. "Perhaps Oliver and I can help you find it."

Goodfellow looked toward me and frowned. His voice became

louder, with an undertone of anger. "What? Well, no thank you, Sam. There's no need to bother. It's not that important, and if I don't find it tonight, perhaps I will another day."

"When did you lose this whatever-it-is?" Sam asked.

Goodfellow looked at us uncertainly. "Well, I'm not sure. Perhaps this morning when I walked down here after church. I noticed the loss later, you see."

Staples nodded and dipped his hand into his pocket. He withdrew it quickly and opened his hand to the suspect selectman. "Is this what you're looking for, Mr. Goodfellow?"

Goodfellow's mouth opened without a sound as he stared. The watch now dangled in a swinging arc held in the sheriff's hand.

"What is that?" the man said. "Is that a watch you hold there? Well, yes, confound it, I *have* lost my watch. Where did you find it, Sam?"

"It was clutched in the hand of Miss Hetta Bird, the old woman found murdered here yesterday morning," Staples lied, making no attempt to hand it over. "Now how do you account for that, sir?"

A hoarse but strangely familiar voice sounded from the shadowy trees behind us. "It was him done it," the supernatural voice croaked. "I seen him do her in."

Goodfellow gasped. "What? What? Who is that? Is this some kind of a joke?"

Staples and I stood there looking at him as he craned his head to peer into the dark woods. He was shaking his head, unable to speak, when there came another sound, this a most unearthly wail. It came from the water's edge, and as we stared, a dim, ghostly figure emerged from the misty pond and walked slowly toward us. It was wearing a long, hooded shroud, and one arm stretched upward holding an open parasol.

It was a woman's voice that sounded spectrally then. "Why have you killed me?" she wailed. "Why have you done this foul thing to me?"

Goodfellow stared horrified at this ghostly form wearing a flowing skirt of rags and wet boots. He moaned, tottered, and then fainted to the ground.

Charley had materialized at my side. "She overdid it, don't you think? I thought mine was better."

Goodfellow lay sprawled on his back, his eyelids fluttering. Margaret Roberts had divested herself of the shroud and stood at my side shivering.

"You didn't tell me that water was so cold," she said. "What took you so long?"

"We had to befuddle him," I said. Then I lifted the lantern close to his face. "Is this the man you saw at your cigar store in Boston?"

She stared down and shook her head. "No, but I have seen the man."

"In the thickets?" Charley asked. "The man you said attacked you?"

She shook her head again. "No, I said it was too dark to see him. It was another time, another place."

Sheriff Staples was growling under his breath. "Will you tell us, please, miss, what you have seen or know of this man?" he asked with impatience.

"He was on the same train that took me from Boston to here," she said. "He was most obnoxious, accosting me, trying to draw me into conversation. I told him he was a vile, noxious old man, and to be gone."

The prostrate Goodfellow fluttered his eyes open. He stared up into the disapproving eyes of Margaret.

"Vixen," he croaked. "Whore of Babylon! I thought I had killed you for rebuffing my attentions!"

Charley and I smiled at each other as Staples began declaiming words of a proper order. "In the name of the state of Massachusetts, and the county of Middlesex, by virtue of the authority vested in me, I do declare you, Gordon Goodfellow, accused of murder, and under said authority will herewith take you into my custody."

The following morning I went to Walden Pond to see Thoreau again, to tell him of the outcome. With his permission, I said, proper credit would be given him in our newspaper.

"I am sure that I never read any memorable news in a newspaper," he said. "If we read of one man robbed, or murdered, or killed by accident, or one house burned, or one vessel wrecked, or one steamboat blown up, or one cow run over on the Western Railroad, or one mad dog killed, or one lot of grasshoppers in the winter—we never need read of another. One is enough."

"Well, yes," I said, "but—"

He continued without notice of my interruption. "If you are acquainted with the principle, what do you care for a myriad instances and applications? To a philosopher, all *news*, as it is called, is gossip, and they who edit and read it are old women over their tea. Yet not a few are greedy after this gossip. There was such a rush, as I hear, the other day at one of the offices to learn the foreign news by the last arrival, that several large squares of plate glass belonging to the establishment were broken by the pressure, news which I seriously think a ready wit might write a twelvemonth or twelve years, beforehand with sufficient accuracy . . ."

It was his habit, as I have noted, to go on at some length about any matter that might otherwise have been passed over without notice.

Nevertheless, I thanked Thoreau, but his mind was already elsewhere.